£2.80

Dedalus Europe 2001
General Editor: Mike Mitchell

Androids from Milk

GW00600652

Eugen Egner

$\mathscr{A}$ndroids from $\mathscr{M}$ilk

Translated by Mike Mitchell

Dedalus

Funded by
THE
ARTS
COUNCIL
OF ENGLAND

Published in the UK by Dedalus Ltd, Langford Lodge, St Judith's Lane, Sawtry, Cambs, PE28 5XE
email: DedalusLimited@compuserve.com

ISBN 1 903517 02 8

Dedalus is distributed in the United States by SCB Distributors, 15608 South New Century Drive, Gardena, California 90248
email: info@scbdistributors.com   web site: www.scbdistributors.com

Dedalus is distributed in Australia & New Zealand by Peribo Pty Ltd, 58 Beaumont Road, Mount Kuring-gai N.S.W. 2080
email: peribo@bigpond.com

Dedalus is distributed in Canada by Marginal Distribution, Unit 102, 277 George Street North, Peterborough, Ontario, KJ9 3G9
email: marginal@marginalbook.com   web site: www.marginal.com

Dedalus is distributed in Italy by Apeiron Editoria & Distribuzione, Localita Pantano, 00060 Sant'Oreste (Roma)
email: grt@apeironbookservice   web site: apeironbookservice.com

First published in German in 1999
First published by Dedalus in 2001

Androiden auf Milchbasis © copyright Haffmans Verlag AG Zurich 1999
Translation copyright © Mike Mitchell 2001

The right of Eugen Egner to be identified as the author and Mike Mitchell to be identified as the translator of this work has been asserted by them in accordance with the Copyright, Designs and Patents Act, 1988.

Typeset by RefineCatch Limited, Bungay, Suffolk
Printed in Finland by WS Bookwell

A C.I.P. listing for this book is available on request.

THE AUTHOR

Eugen Egner (born 1951) has found fame in Germany as both a writer and a graphic artist, especially for his cartoons and illustrations.

He has written short radio plays plus short stories and novels including *Cosmic Flip*, *From the Diary of an Alcoholic*, *When Father Christmas was Mother Christmas*, *The Diaries of WA Mozart* and *The Artificial Man*.

His style of writing has been described as anarchic fantasy.

THE TRANSLATOR

Mike Mitchell is one of Dedalus's editorial directors and is responsible for the Dedalus translation programme. His publications include *The Dedalus Book of Austrian Fantasy*, *Peter Hacks: Drama for a Socialist Society* and *Austria* in the *World Bibliographical Series*.

Mike Mitchell's translations include all the novels of Gustav Meyrink, three by Herbert Rosendorfer, *The Great Bagarozy* by Helmut Krausser and *Simplicissimus* by Grimmelshausen; his latest is *Poems and Plays* by Oskar Kokoschka.

His translation of Rosendorfer's *Letters Back to Ancient China* won the 1998 Schegel-Tieck German Translation Prize.

Author's Preface

I wrote this book in less than two hours. I think I've made as much of it as one could in such a short time.

Corrected Author's Preface

This book is a word-for-word record of what my wife said in her sleep last night.

Second Corrected Author's Preface

Enchanted by the unexpected beauty of fish, I bought one. After a few days it started to go through various stages of evolution. Eventually it crawled onto dry land and developed into a bird, a bird that was sitting on a branch yesterday singing this book, right down to the very last word.

Third Corrected Author's Preface

Sailing the snake-like seas with Admiral von Schwein-erey, one day we picked up a message in a bottle. It took us a long time to get the tape cassette out of the bottle without breaking the latter. What follows is an exact transcript of what was recorded on the tape.

Fourth Corrected Author's Preface

Once again, following my usual habit, I had begun to 'make the garment by guesstimation, starting out from one cuff', as Arno Schmidt puts it in his 'Dickens Dialogue', *Tom All Alone's*. I had no idea what to write, but my desire to write *something* was overpowering. So I used a couple of bits I stole from Flamel and Péret to get me going. Still being at a loss, I mixed in any autobiographical details that occurred to me, as well as everything I was fascinated by at that moment. Stirring the ingredients soon made my head and my writing hand ache. Countless times the bullshit was changed, rearranged and written out again. At some point it reached that long-awaited stage at which the hotchpotch developed its own momentum, adding its own two-penn'orth to the evolving manuscript. After two months I had finally managed to put twenty pages together. I – a little man with weak nerves – even had a kind of plan for the next stages of my plot! Everything seemed to be turning out fine. Then one morning I succumbed to a particularly virulent bout of despair and tore up the manuscript, together with all my notes, into tiny pieces. And to save myself the humiliation, should I later come to regret this action, of painstakingly gluing the fragments back together again, I immediately consigned the lot to the household rubbish in the dustbin behind the house. And there it stayed. In two days' time it would be smoke coming out of the chimney of the council incinerator.

Lying in bed on my problem hair that night, I couldn't get to sleep. I was surprised how well I could remember the manuscript, which had now as good as departed this material world. I felt a terrible urge to reconstruct the whole thing from memory. At once I became conscious of spatial, geographical factors: whilst the manuscript had, until a short time ago, been in a blue folder on my desk some ten or twelve metres to the south-west of my bed, it was now about five or six metres to the east, outside in the dustbin, and in a considerably altered state.

During the night the local alley-cats stole my torn-up manuscript from the rubbish container. They argued violently over the rights to it, the cater-wauling was horrible. The fat black tom who, thanks to his superior body weight, emerged victorious from the spat, would surely have published my rejected manuscript under his own name if the woman where he lived had not found it and taken it away from him.[1] Equipped by nature with prehensile hands, she found it much easier than her cat to employ a tube of all-purpose glue to stick his spoils together. As I have already mentioned, the manuscript had developed a certain inner momentum and continued to grow more or less under its own steam, so that this book is the product of those original twenty pages. That I

[1] I wonder what would have happened if my cat, which also took part in the fracas, had been triumphant and returned home with my literary paperchase?

appear on the title-page as author is one of life's little ironies.

When the woman read what she had stuck together, she chucked the restored pages into the box of waste paper in annoyance, without tearing them up first. The manuscript spent several weeks lying underneath old newspapers, brochures and empty soap packets, and just grew. Eventually the pile of waste paper became too high and the woman took it to the skip. What exactly happened next I can't now remember. Perhaps she arrived there at the same time as I did, so that I recognised my handwriting among her waste paper and took out page after page, tears in my eyes, or perhaps I, having renounced literature and trying to earn some cash by other means, happened to get a job with a paper-recycling firm where, to my surprise, I came across my manuscript. Whatever the precise course of events, the fact is that, in some way or other, I found it again. It was still growing. I did nothing to stop it. As soon as it was fully grown, I sent it to the publishers, who brought it out in the form you have in your hands.

Eugen Egner, winter 1998

Preliminaries

My parents had long white beards. I inherited one of them, probably a cross between the two, which I keep in a drawer of my casket.

It was my parents' original intention for me to qualify for the position of official illustrator. Even as a small child I had demonstrated my artistic talent by, for example, creating lyrical inscriptions on vehicles with my bare hands and independently inventing coloured pencils, paper and a process for making cartoon films. That was why my parents destined me for the career of official illustrator. That is, initially I was even supposed to become an official *painter*. Since time immemorial painting had been more highly regarded than drawing, involving as it does the transfer of official portraits or scenes onto canvas by means of oil paints, and not onto paper by means of pencils, pens or water colours. It was hallowed by tradition. As far as social and artistic status were concerned, official painters stood as far above official illustrators as oil paint is thicker than water colour. However, since I was of a delicate constitution it was decided the work, which is mostly carried out standing up at an easel, would be too strenuous for me. It also seemed unlikely that I would be able to hold the heavy palette for long. I was doubtless better suited to an activity that could be done sitting down with lightweight equipment. But before I could begin my training as official illustrator I was distracted from the graphic arts.

On the very day when I had created a full-colour handbook of medicine entirely on my own (this would have scarcely been possible if I had not beforehand been given the fantastic school paint-box as an offering from the parish priest), on the evening of that day, then, my father came home from work on the monkey farm and brought me my first records. Lovingly he unwrapped them from his long white beard. My mother stopped ironing her long white beard on the kitchen table and came to join us. Being still young, I was the only one without a beard.

These marvellous records, so-called 'forty-fives' or 'singles', were from liquidation or remaindered stock. My father had acquired them from the record store for a relatively small sum. According to the label, these first discs in my life contained recordings of a singer by the name of Canicula Karnivora, and probably came from the other side. But the most marvellous part was when my father ruffled up his long white beard and, to our amazement (I think even he was a little amazed himself), pulled out a fully operational radiogram. It was almost like giving birth, except the procedure was completely dry and clean, apart from the amount of perspiration appropriate to the weight of the object. My medical handbook was completely forgotten, the wind carried it off, page by page. With immediate effect, playing records was what counted in our household. My parents quickly calmed down (they had their beards, of course), but I became more and more twitchy and fidgety. From now on the fine arts could 'get stuffed', as I put it. Records were my life. I no longer had to go outside at sunset every evening to whistle along to the neighbours' radio music blaring from every window until I collapsed in exhaustion on the doorstep, cheeks drooping with fatigue, lips still pursed but soundless and useless. And of course it was also nicer for the neighbours that my dreaded evening concerts stopped. I spent all my time sitting by the radiogram listening to records, the number of which constantly increased.

With time I became an older, heavier and, I think one could say, a writer person. After all, over the years I had written several books, all of which were about records. I used the money they brought in to buy more records, which I then described in further books. To get hold of more records, I even started writing reviews for specialist magazines. At my very first attempt I managed to review a hundred and twenty random discs in half a page. My piece began, 'If you want, you can buy this or that record,' and didn't improve as it went on. They refused to pay for the hundred and twenty review discs and there was no question of a fee. The publisher, who had wanted to build me up as a house author, was no longer prepared to publish my eternal record books. My work was criticised as being 'mere disc literature'. Unashamed, I countered:

'Let people call me Discman Egner if they want. I'm proud of it. Records play a very important role in our society, in our economy. It is a sector which

registers higher annual profits than the entire ship-
building and chocolate industries combined. And
as for the criticism that what I write is 'mere disc
literature', are authors of other genres accused of
writing, say, 'mere gun literature' or 'mere genital
literature'? And if they were, would those bum-
fiddlers have the balls to stand up and declare they
were proud of their genre? In our world records are
as widespread as guns or genitals, so no one should
be surprised if they give rise to a literature of their
own.'

I was banned from writing. All the books I had
written disappeared from the market within a short
time. My name was erased from the history of literature. Deprived of my source of income overnight, I
was compelled to sell off my gigantic private record
library. After two years I had to return to the room I
had had as a boy in my parents' house. Indigence was
my lot.

One late afternoon in May a gang of male juvenile
delinquents invaded our suburban street. They
advanced at a steady pace, each carrying in one hand
a stack of records initially reaching from navel to
chin; with the other hand they took one disc after
another and hurled them at the houses on either side
of the street. Risking my life, I observed the scene
from the window. Actually it was quite jolly to see
the records land on the sloping roofs and then shoot
off, as if from a ski jump, up into the sky, where
they damaged several aeroplanes. When records
plunge down from a great height, all you can do is
pray, and even that's not much use. A dachshund

that had for years suffered from convulsive barking and the owner-operator of an open-air sawmill were both abruptly decapitated.

Some of the discs flew over the roofs and came down on the other side. Later, when the discus-throwing horde had proceeded on its way, not only the street, pavement and front gardens were strewn with records, but also the gardens and lawns behind the houses.

Since I was urgently in need of exercise and air, I plucked up all my courage and went to where the dustbins stood in enemy territory at the back of the house. Desolate it was and dire, completely exposed to the evil eye of the neighbourhood. The sun was already setting, by now it was November. Once again the concrete garden tried to murder me with the mere sight of it. I couldn't spend more than ten minutes in that place or my cerebral self-image might go on the blink and I would come to regard myself as a completely different person. The shortage of oxygen caused by the concrete prevents certain cells in my brain from restraining other cells to the desired extent and thus producing the balance that creates reality. Any moment I could suffer an outbreak of hyperactivity! 'I' already suspected 'I' was 'mother-of-fur's coat in a school-age universe'. Close to disintegration, what was left of me hastily gathered up the records lying on our property.

With no enthusiasm whatsoever, either. Fictional astronauts on planets for whose conditions they have not been adapted probably grope around like me behind my parents' house. If I could have bottled myself up in a thermos flask by exerting my spiritual power, I would have done so. I tried to go back into the house through the wall, but without success. There was nothing for it but to take the 'hell's-gate path' along the completely unprotected gable end of the house round to the front, where I hoped to be able to reach the brutally exposed door. The whole of my route was laid with concrete slabs. Steps suddenly appeared on which I almost broke my neck. On either side my *via dolorosa* was bounded by vertical concrete slabs, some bedded in the soil, others bolted to the house wall. I no longer had any idea whether my great-grandfather had possessed a flourishing schnapps factory or whether I, in the form of two girls, was on my way to Hutter's floating castle. The moon looked on, grumbling. At my great-grandfather's request, we two girls would have described it as follows:

'A reasonably round, shining white disc within a square outline set on one corner (the sides of the square corresponding to the diameter of the disc), surrounded by a bluish corona consisting of three superimposed haloes arranged in a pyramid.'

In the garden it had still been November. When I entered the ancestral home and felt myself again, it was already the third Sunday in advent. The speed at which time was passing was enough to make you feel sick. If someone, for example, simply went to dry his hands on a tree trunk, he would discover afterwards that a month had passed. It was temporal inflation and inhibited any kind of activity. A year was no longer worth anything. This observation made no claim to originality. It was nothing new at all. The ancients themselves, in particular the Delawares, had made a song and dance about it. Eventually the latter had no time left at all for singing or dancing, nor even for existing, and had to call in the receivers (who, it is said, found hardly any objects worth distraining, 'mainly junk'). The liquidation of the bankrupt Delaware estate provided the raw materials for the aforementioned schnapps factory my great-grandfather set up in 1890.

It is a well-known fact that schnapps, especially when drunk, contributes to the devaluation of time. A schnapps drinker has no time for anything else. There have been some who had just enough time to down their first glass and were already dying of old age as they poured themselves a second. Many didn't even have enough time to become alcoholics.

Carrying the records, an impressive stack, I reached my room just in time for Christmas. I let down the blinds. In the dark I managed to find an old radiogram, and once I'd switched on the radio and lifted the lid of the record-player I could see something at last. The dial and the record-playing compartment, with its light that functioned like that of a refrigerator, gave off a warm, yellowish glow. This 'magic eye', so beloved of older writers on radio, added to the ambience. I decided listening to the records I had found was worthy of celebration, so I went to my parents' kitchen and had a look in the fridge. There was a three-quarter-full litre bottle of white wine with a note stuck to it:

Dear son,
Please drink the wine before it goes off.
  Best wishes,
    Your parents

P.S. We've sold the house so we can start a new life
somewhere else. The parish priest will look after
you.

I wanted to listen to my records and drink the
wine before the new owner or the parish priest
turned up. I picked up the first one. The label said
'Praisedame Boarbones', performed by 'The Flesh-
eating Fetish Bitches'. The record was desperate to
come to life, so I played it and emptied a glass.
Immediately I was sorry I couldn't write about the
disc, I found it so wonderfully sensitising. The little
light on the radiogram was witness to my search for
the secret women hiding somewhere in the room. In
order to fortify myself sufficiently for this, I emptied
the bottle. But then I didn't have the strength left to
put on another record. I left after-images around the
room; wherever I had been, I left my image. I
climbed onto the shoulders of one of them straightaway. Wasn't there a concealed door somewhere in
the ceiling? Could I perhaps just push my hand
through it like paper? If not, could I not screw the
records to it?
Then there was a knock at the door. The after-
image on whose shoulders I was standing faded and I
crashed to the floor. My mother burst into the room
like a land-reform act. They had cancelled the sale of

the house. That's the way my parents were, that's the way they'd always been.

'I've just beaten your father in our UHT-milk-drinking contest,' my mother announced. 'But you shouldn't be lying on the floor. Go to bed early instead. Tomorrow you have to finish another picture.'

'Another picture? What other picture?'

'Perhaps you would have the goodness to remember that we are paying for your training as an official illustrator.'

'Oh, you're paying for me to retrain . . .'

'Retrain? What's got into you? We've been trying to get you qualified for that for the last twenty years.'

'But I was a record-writer. They used to call me . . .'

'You're just trying to provoke me! Off you go to bed now. Tomorrow is the last day you can send off your picture. You've left everything till the last moment again. You should be ashamed of yourself.'

She went out of the room.

I was in shock. My parents had been making me train as an official illustrator for twenty years? No. That wasn't me. That was someone else. Someone who didn't look like me at all and had a different name.

You have entered the sphere of fatality of your own free will, now be patient and compliant.

Wieniedikt Jerofieyew, *The Journey to Petushky*

I

For twenty years they had persuaded Reuben Hecht that he was studying official illustration at the Holy German Paintbrush Distance Learning Academy in Brunswick.

Reuben Hecht hated drawing. He would never have bothered with it if his parents hadn't intended him for the career of official illustrator in the Colony.

At the age of seventeen Reuben had been registered for the correspondence course by his ambitious father. Initially, and for reasons of prestige, he had been meant to follow a course in official *painting*. But the pictures that had appeared on his grounds had given no grounds for hope, it always ended in smears and tears. When he had discovered, while getting undressed one night, that the oil-paint had even got on his underclothes, he had run away there and then under cover of darkness. An equally runaway passenger train had taken him to the Ivory Coast. The conductor gave him an address in Abidjan where other defectors from the Holy German Paintbrush Distance Learning Academy were living. Hardly had he arrived, though, than Reuben discovered that Africa was not for him. The misery of exile struck him a violent blow and he collapsed in a heap. When he came to again, he was at home in his bed. His parents said nothing about his having been away. To be on the safe side, he didn't enquire about it either. The diagnosis of Dr Rossman, the family doctor, was that Reuben had been infected with 'some fancy tropical disease or other' as a consequence of which he would stay seventeen years old for all time. But how had he got home? Had his parents come to fetch him in their car, or had perhaps a bearded man in a diving suit pushed him all the way back in a wheelchair? It was something that was never mentioned. However, at least his parents arranged for him to be excused painting; since then he had been studying official illustration.

His father, the noted anthropologist Lehmann Hecht, had spent a considerable time in the Colony, pursuing his research. Since time out of mind the country had been subjugated and exploited by any and every ruffian who happened along. After many centuries of overuse it was completely worn out, cracked and crumbling, thin and threadbare, everything looked pale and coarse, all objects had thick white shadows down their left side. Since the country was now no use at all, before they marched in the new rulers had pulled it off like an old blanket. A new, pristine land had been revealed with a new, inscrutable mode of reality that the occupying power could not come to grips with. The nature of the aboriginal population (Lehmann Hecht's field of research) was never established. They all looked like women, with fair hair and fair complexions. Both sexes appeared to have female characteristics. It was assumed the taller ones were the women. A further astonishing phenomenon was the fact that in the Colony optical lenses were completely ineffective. The unavailability of photographic evidence meant that conditions there were absolutely ante-Daguerrian. For the purposes of documentation they were compelled to revert entirely to the atavistic means of brush, pen and pencil. One could go far as an official illustrator, never mind as an official painter.

A few months previously, Hecht's father had returned from the Colony a broken man who had undergone a strange psychological mutation. Since then he kept on challenging his wife to UHT-milk-drinking contests, and because he was so often beaten, he had taken to his bed, where he stayed. At first the State Institute for Primate Research – they were, after all, his employers – had rung up to ask whether he didn't fancy coming back to work.

'The primates can go fuck themselves, I'm hatching out a dwarf,' had been Lehmann Hecht's reply. With every day that passed he became more bedridden.

'Your husband has completely fused with his bed,' Dr Rossman had told Frau Hecht a few days ago. 'How long has he been lying there?'

Rossman was the town medical officer of health and she had to tell him something or he wouldn't go away. He was already getting a bit fractious.

'Out with it, then! Otherwise I'll give you an injection! With ice-cold hands! Or I'll have you abducted by extra-terrestrials for their experiments. Well then? How long has he been lying there?'

Hecht's mother improvised. 'With retrospective effect, for ten years, Dr Rossman.'

'That's more than seven months! And for what purpose, may I ask?'

'To hatch out a dwarf, doctor.'

'No shit!' bellowed Rossman. 'Well blow my nose and call me Pope!'

He downed a small bottle of medicine to celebrate the success of his interrogation and wrapped the shower-curtain more tightly round him.

'I can't tell you how we're going to get him out of there just at the moment. We might have to use dynamite, but that could cost us all our lives. You'll hear from me when the time comes. Don't call me, I'll call you.'

He left. For a time his iron snow-shovel could still be heard scratching round the house, then he was gone.

On the Friday morning Reuben Hecht woke up around seven o'clock. Immediately he remembered his correspondence course.

'Oh dear!' He remembered something else. 'And I'm going to have to die some day as well.'

He struggled out of bed, his breakfast went all wrong. He was afraid he'd be committed to Frau Suse's clinic sooner or later. Most of the patients there were people who had lost all confidence in their thin, sparse locks and poor hairstyles. Attached to the clinic was a fairy-tale theme park.

There was nothing worse for Reuben Hecht than having to be present while he was drawing. For him it was just a continuation of the painting he loathed by other means. His pet hate was the theory of perspective. Before the submission date his mother regularly had to supervise his work, wooden spoon at the ready. He had been the ruin of countless vanishing points and wooden spoons. No help was to be expected from outside, neither from the parish priest nor the family GP.

This was the way things had been for twenty years. Reuben was still seventeen, one was considerably the worse for wear, one's hair was a mess.

What Reuben Hecht in fact did not know was that he was just being used to produce free illustrations for an uncouth handbook of medicine (indeed, his parents were paying for him to do so). This handbook was the life's work of the director of the Holy German Paintbrush Distance Learning Academy in Brunswick, Professor Mothorheym. Everything the professor did was directed solely towards completing this work and seeing it through the press. He didn't care if it took twenty years or more to finish, even if the publishing house where it was to appear had grown impatient and was urging him to hurry up. So that his student would not realise that he was illustrating an uncouth handbook of medicine, his exercises were disguised with pretend titles:

- *Draw a portrait of Arno Schmidt explaining prairie-quality card indexes to the Mohicans whilst Alice is chopping wood on his head.*
- *Draw a bearded Eskimo.*
- *Draw some dried extra-terrestrials with* peau d'orange.

According to Professor Mothorheym's covert intentions, these ought to result in pictures of illnesses and their symptoms. (In the case of the three examples given above: 'Inflammation of the tuber', 'Hirsutism among B-class juveniles', 'Poor general health'.)

Around midday Reuben's exasperation boiled over. 'It's getting worse with every line!' he screamed.

During the last three hours he had completely ruined several formerly white sheets of cartridge paper, using huge amounts of opaque white in the process, and there was still no sign of anything remotely approximating to the task as set. By now he was almost too weak to tear his final sheet of cartridge paper up into pieces. He felt the last dregs of the courage he needed to face up to life hop on its scooter and hightail it into the distance, and there was not a thing he could do to stop it. Almost a broken man like his father, though without his bizarre psychological mutation, he dragged himself to the kitchen, where his mother was trying to prepare their midday meal. She was staring through thick clouds of smoke at the ashes of the frying pan, which she doused with UHT milk. Reuben quickly realised there was no hope of a hot meal. The kitchen had to be abandoned. Mother and son escaped to the living room where some ageing pretzels were extracted from the sideboard. While consuming these emergency rations, Reuben asked his parent and guardian, 'May I go to the Flesh-eating Fetish Bitches' concert tomorrow evening?'

He had been seventeen for twenty years, and he

had spent the whole week expunging every stroke of Indian ink he put onto paper with copious amounts of opaque white. He was surely due some weekend recreation appropriate to his age! His social life was problematical enough as it was. Friends who had formerly been of the same age were now, assuming they were still alive, thirty-somethings with neither time nor use for him. It didn't seem worthwhile going to the trouble of acquiring a new circle of acquaintances every few years who would then proceed to outgrow him. Twenty years ago he'd had a penfriend, an English girl. Their correspondence had been conducted in such passionate terms that she had had a baby. And that had been the end of the epistolary affair. Reuben had never heard from the English girl again, nor ever seen his daughter.

He was welcome to go to the Flesh-eating Fetish Bitches' concert tomorrow evening, his mother decreed, where he could scream himself hoarse and jig about in the aisle to his heart's content. However, this Friday afternoon, she said, he had to pop out and replenish their supplies of opaque white and wooden spoons. The only shop open for miles around was the petrol station on the corner. As the sole way of getting to the petrol station was up a steep flight of steps, relatively few cars made use of the facility.

The manageress appeared to be a beautiful Ethiopian woman with elflocks reaching down to her backside. She was right out of opaque white and wooden spoons. Even the petrol-station dog couldn't sniff out any remnant stock. There was a telex stating that a fresh delivery would arrive next Tuesday. To

cheer him up, the beautiful Ethiopian woman gave
Reuben a marzipan bar. It sent icy shivers down his
spine when he imagined what it would be like if the
Hechts should run out of opaque white and wooden
spoons on the very afternoon a drawing was due and
had to be got to the post office before it closed at all
costs. All attempts to produce home-made opaque
white by thickening UHT milk with various sub-
stances such as custard powder, heroin or plaster of
Paris had failed. And Frau Hecht would not know
what to lay into her son with.

Reuben pictured pallid blondes taking him in a
white minibus to the nearest town, where he hoped
he might find opaque white and wooden spoons. Why
such an idea should occur to him became clear as
soon as he left the shop. Outside, four pallid blondes,
having refuelled their white minibus, were just carrying it down the steep steps. Reuben, immediately
attracted by their pale charms, rushed over to help
them. At the bottom of the steps they thanked him,
claiming to be the Flesh-eating Fetish Bitches.
Reuben was not a little surprised at this. These four
young ladies looked very models of Teutonic woman-
dom as proclaimed by Third-Reich Aryanomanes,
though lacking – thank God! – the silly-girl-next-
door expressions mandatory for Strength-through-
Joy maidens. But the Flesh-eating Fetish Bitches,
whom he had seen in photographs and on television,
were unkempt, half-naked, red- and black-haired
viragoes in weird outfits.

'But you don't look at all like yourselves,' he
protested.

'Well,' they said, 'this's the way we happen to look in our private lives.'

They said goodbye and gave him a complimentary ticket for the next evening's concert, also promising, 'We're going to send you a magic token. Have a good look at your private parts tomorrow morning.'

'OK, yeah, great,' was Reuben's stupid response. What he thought was, 'Hope it's not a skin disease. Who knows what their sense of humour's like.'

Back home he played all the Flesh-eating Fetish Bitches' records one after the other.

'It can't be those four at the petrol station,' he thought every time he looked at the photographs of the rock group on the record sleeves. He spent the rest of the day listening to them; the night he spent in the pyjamas he still had from the moonlanding.

He woke up at seven next morning. Immediately he thought of the concert he was going to that evening and recalled his meeting with the pallid blondes the previous day.

'Oh yes, and they were going to send me a magic token too,' he remembered.

As prophesied, Reuben found something where he had his genitals, those things that are usually cut off by people who are too stupid or too lazy to wash themselves down there: one long, loose, blond hair. Just the kind of hair the four young women had.

'How did they do that?' he wondered.

That it must have come from them was beyond doubt. Reuben himself was dark-haired, as were his parents, and he didn't know any other blond people. Meditatively he placed the hair in a tin cigarette box.

His idea was to keep the mysterious relic in his desk, but he was so overcome with amazement he mistook his jacket for the latter and put the tin in his inside pocket.

That afternoon his father, totally ignoring the fact that he was fused to the sheets and without having hatched out a dwarf, got up from his bed. He went down to the cellar and turned off the water for the whole house. Then he took off every tap and pumped air into the pipes. Finally he screwed the taps back on and turned the mains stopcock in the cellar on again.

There was a deafening racket, as if salvoes of machine-gun fire were being let off inside the walls. In addition, there was a terrifying rumbling and roaring, the walls seemed about to explode at any moment. Frau Hecht screamed that she was going to seek asylum with the council environmental health services, her husband announced he was going to hang himself.

Unnoticed by either, Reuben donned some pointed shoes, threw on his jacket and left. All around on the estate people were shaking with contentment. Circular shields on the outer walls of each house captured signals from the cosmos which brought purpose to the lives of the people in their sitting rooms, even gave meaning to their whole existence. On the wall inside every home, alongside portraits of John F. Kennedy, the Pope and Elvis Presley, hung coloured likenesses of the head of government, a politician who, after a good dozen years in office, had attained the wisdom and beauty of ripe old age. He had a gracious smile on his face; behind him the heavens were opening wide.

As by far the longest-serving seventeen-year-old in the town, Reuben intended to travel incognito. The journey should only cost seventy pfennigs and the buses were decorated with even more pine boughs and fairy lights than at Christmas. He couldn't wait to meet the Flesh-eating Fetish Bitches again. There were so many things he needed to ask. What was all this about the hair? And how come they looked completely different in private from their photos? He just had to talk to them before the concert. In that case it would be a good idea to arrive at the venue in plenty of time. He decided to buy a bouquet of roses for the cleaner to get her to let him into the artistes' dressing-room. If that didn't do the trick, he'd have to throw stones at her, but he'd rather not think about that.

The bus-stop, a regular bus-station-with-soup-kitchen-attached, was a reasonable distance from the family home. A quiet and inconspicuous gang of bikers clad in black leathers were standing beside the bus-shelter. The women among them were as beautiful as Snow White, and as pale. When Reuben walked past in his pointed shoes they raised their crash-helmets politely. Immediately opposite, its doors wide open, the number 48 with its beer-cellar was waiting. At that moment the bikers' leader came clattering up the stairs, accompanied by three bus-drivers.

'Right,' she squealed in a jolly, girlish voice, 'one for the road with you lot and then it's off to the concert.'

45

So they all turned on their heels and went back down to the beer-cellar. The whole bus wobbled while they were drinking their beer. Reuben was pleased to be in such an interesting place instead of sitting at home with his problem parents, spending the evening drawing. It was the best thing that could happen to a seventeen-year-old, no more and no less.

But every silver lining has to have a cloud. As Reuben was standing there enjoying himself, he heard Dr Rossman's iron snow-shovel scraping along the bus-station tarmac. The sound was getting nearer. Suddenly Rossman came round the corner of the bus-shelter.

'Hands up,' he shouted, when he discovered Reuben. A moment later his bosom friend, Prümers the parish priest, appeared from the same direction.

'Reuben Hecht!' screamed Prümers. 'Is this the company you keep? Shame on you to bring such disgrace on your poor, poor parents!'

'Even in death they are not spared,' added Rossman.

'Come and repent,' cried Prümers.

The medical officer of health was getting worked up. 'Just look what you've done!' he exclaimed.

'But I haven't done anything at all,' protested Reuben, flabbergasted. 'I've no idea what you're on about. My parents know I'm going to the concert this evening.'

'To a concert!' squawked Prümers. 'To worship the devil, you mean! And with your parents laid out at home, cold and dead!'

'Cold and dead!' repeated Rossman, at which Prümers yowled, 'Amen, amen, amen.'

Reuben was beginning to feel ill. His irritable bowel syndrome had been aroused and the point fell off one of his shoes. What on earth were these two lunatics talking about?

By now Rossman was foaming at the mouth. 'And you weren't at home to lend those to whom you owe everything – I repeat: *everything* – your aid in their hour of need! Instead you're hanging around the bus-station!'

'That can cost you your eternal bliss, no problem!' exulted the priest. 'You didn't honour your father and mother, you shit! You should be sold off to a laboratory where they do animal experiments.'

'He has to be sent to the children's home, as it is,' Dr Rossman declared, referring to Reuben's inability ever to come of age.

'What do you mean?' Reuben asked. 'What is going on? What are you trying to tell me, for God's sake?'

'"For God's sake"! Just listen to the sinner!' Prümers expostulated. He hit Reuben in the face, but his aim was poor.

'Oh, come on now,' said one of the leather-clad bikers. The others huddled closer together apprehensively. Reuben regretted he had no firearm with him.

'You shall not take the name of the Lord your God in your mouth!' hissed Prümers. 'Especially not *you* of all people!'

'You want to know what's going on, do you?' Rossman bawled at the boy. 'I'll tell you what's going

47

on. After all, I am the doctor who signed the death certificates. Your father strung himself up and your mother was so fed up with the whole business, she just dropped down dead.'

Reuben went pale with shock. 'It must have all happened very quickly,' he said. 'I've only been away for fifteen minutes at the most . . .'

'Smart-arse!' Rossman roared, threatening Reuben with his snow-shovel. 'Are you questioning my competence? Or my credibility? Just you wait and see what's going to happen next!'

'In the name of the Father, the Son and the Holy Ghost,' intoned Prümers in support.

'We're taking you to the children's home right away and we'll leave you there to rot,' Rossman decreed.

The two crackpots grabbed the weedy boy roughly and started tugging at him.

Just then the leader of the bikers came back up the cellar steps, accompanied by the three bus-drivers. One glance at the scene was enough.

'Leave the lad alone at once,' she ordered Rossman and Prümers, this time speaking in a loud, deep voice.

'You keep out of this, bikers' slut!' replied the medical officer of health, 'or I'll have you put down.'

'From top to toe!' added the priest.

The three bus-drivers' red noses dilated, their shaggy moustaches bristled. They stepped on the accelerators in their shoes until they really got themselves going. When they had finished with Rossman and Prümers, the pair were no longer Rossman and

Prümers, but Harprecht and Herkenrath. Once their bruises and scratch marks had healed up they'd have to apply to the registry office for new identity cards. The chain-smoking official with her mile-long finger-nails would give them such a hard time, they'd wish they'd never been born. The bikers knew that as well and sniggered gloatingly. Harprecht and Herkenrath fled on the iron snow-shovel, now twisted into a grotesque shape.

One should not humiliate people of a malicious disposition and let them continue to live. History is bursting at the seams with examples demonstrating the truth of this statement. It was no different in the cases of the former Herr Rossman and the former Herr Prümers. From that point on, like true funda-mentalists, they directed all their energies towards putting Reuben in the children's home. Their bound-less hatred was the one thing keeping them alive; if ever they achieved their aim they would immediately subside into senility and die an OAP's death.

Reuben was mightily relieved to be rid of the two lunatics. Shyly he thanked the bus-drivers, but they waved his expressions of gratitude aside. 'Not at all, not at all. Three against two, no sweat.'

The bikers' leader cried in a high-pitched voice, 'As a reward I'll have one last beer with you.'

Like Pavlov's dogs, the four of them immediately scuttled back down to the beer cellar of the number 48.

Reuben wondered whether what he had been told about his parents was true or not. All things con-sidered, it seemed rather unlikely they would commit suicide without so much as a by-your-leave the moment he left the house. The fact that of all people it was the medical officer of health and the parish priest who had brought the news he saw as a further argument against it. But ought he perhaps to take the precaution of going home to make sure? All the way back home? Harprecht and Herkenrath could well be lying in wait for him somewhere along the route. Furthermore, if he did go there and his parents really were dead, he was certain to be pounced on and put in the home.

'This'll be my plan of action,' he decided. 'I won't go straight home after the concert, I'll ring up from town. If my parents answer, I'll just put the phone down and go home. If it's the police or Harprecht and Herkenrath I'll stay in the town and start a new life. If no one answers I'll try three more times during the next hour. If there's still no answer, I'll also start a new life.'

While he was thinking this out he walked up and down. The bikers seemed rather reserved and it was difficult to get into conversation with them. They were still standing in a quiet and inconspicuous group beside the bus-shelter. Some were combing their hair while others were trying to put inscriptions on the back of their leather jackets with bolts and rivets. But what should the inscriptions say? 'Hard-line Hell's Angels Support Peking'? Or 'Angstworm's Phantom Brides, retd.'? No one had any idea and so the operation came to nothing.

It would soon be time for the 48 to leave, Reuben could feel it distinctly. The cooks in the soup-kitchen had the same kind of feeling too. They also thought that Reuben looked hungry. However, before they could offer him a complimentary bowl of soup, a cry came up from the beer-cellar stairs of the number 48, 'The bus hasn't gone yet, thank God!'

'But it must be going to leave any moment now.'

'That's enough of the beer!'

'We're off to the concert.'

The three drivers took their seats next to each other at their instrument panels. The bikers were enticed onto the bus by their leader. But there was a notice banning motorbikes.

'Take them down into the beer-cellar and hang the *Out of beer* sign at the top of the stairs, then the inspectors won't notice,' one of the drivers suggested.

So that's what they did. Finally the Christmas lights were switched on, and with them the engine. When Reuben put his hand in his jacket pocket to get out his purse for the seventy pfennigs conveyance charge, to his great surprise he felt the tin box with the blond hair he'd found that morning. He almost gave a scream because he had assumed it was at home in his desk. As the reader will remember, he had been so confused he had mistaken his jacket for his desk. In contrast to the reader, however, he had never been made aware of his mistake. That was why the unexpected discovery of the box seemed as mysterious to him as the appearance of the alien hair where his private parts were. He wondered whether the four pale women hadn't 'magicked' the tin into his pocket in the same way. That was another thing he would have to ask the Flesh-eating Fetish Bitches.

The bus set off amid the exultant cheers of the cooks from the soup-kitchen. Reuben was sitting right behind the drivers on a seat upholstered in red leather, trying to guess which one was driving. They didn't know themselves. Of the three sets of instruments, only one actually worked, but no one could tell which, as it was a different one each time.

They only picked up passengers who were either going to the concert or were wearing jackets made out of old Persian carpets. Reuben did not join in the conversation with the other passengers. He was much too preoccupied with:

a) everything connected with the blondes at the petrol station, and that was quite a lot in itself;
b) the question as to which of the drivers was actually driving;
c) the scene at the bus-station, including the question of whether his parents were still alive or not;
d) wondering what the leader of the bikers would feel like.

The list was handed round in which each of the passengers wrote down the number of the steering unit they thought was in operation on this journey. Reuben put down number 2 and signed his name beside it. At the end of the journey a red light lit up on the control panel which had actually been in operation. Then the list was checked. There were always some very nice prizes to be won. This time 3 turned out to be the winning number. All the bikers had put that down, so they had to share the prize: a new type of non-toxic drug, that is a pocket appliance emitting radiation at a frequency that worked directly on the electrical impulses of the user's brain. As a consolation prize Reuben was given a tube of 'Dr Wirefather's Special Glue for Broken-off Shoe-tips'. At once everyone else on the bus apart from him was engrossed in the hallucinogenic gadget. Thus it was that he was the only one to get out and go to the concert hall. He wanted nothing to do with drugs, of whatever kind. His life was complicated enough as it was and he had to keep a clear head.

A large, dark-red bus with 'The Flesh-eating Fetish Bitches' written on it was parked outside the stage entrance to the concert hall.

'They presumably only use the white minibus for private purposes,' thought Reuben.

An army of workers was occupied installing the sound-system on the stage. There were three hours to go before the concert started. Reuben asked the stage hands whether the group had already arrived. No, they replied, they only came an hour before the show and would he please get the hell out of there.

Diagonally opposite was a shop specialising in 'Brushes for Carters and Strangers'. To pass the time, Reuben learnt the window display off by heart. He kept on turning round all the time to see if the Flesh-eating Fetish Bitches had arrived yet. That made him feel sick. He had to keep his eyes closed for almost two hours before he felt better again. By that time there was a great crowd queuing at the box office. Fortunately he had his complimentary ticket.

The huge audience was waiting in the foyer and galleries. As he was sliding round on the smooth floor Reuben came across the bikers, who had obviously managed to tear themselves away from the psycho-gadget. They got talking.

'Oh that load of crap. The batteries ran down in two shakes of a biker's tail,' the leader told him. 'I'm sticking to the beer.' The others nodded earnestly.

Reuben asked if the Flesh-eating Fetish Bitches had arrived. As it happened, the bikers' leader was a cousin of the lead guitarist. She had no difficulty taking Reuben backstage and arranging a meeting. As they made their way to the dressing-room he proudly revealed to her that he had already met the ladies in their private capacity.

But the ladies themselves refused to confirm this when they were confronted with him a few moments later.

'We don't know him,' they said.

Although they hadn't finished putting on their stage costumes and doing their make-up, they looked just like their well-known publicity photographs: unkempt, half-naked, red- and black-haired viragoes in weird outfits.

'But you must remember me,' Reuben said. 'Yesterday, at the petrol station . . . You were all as blond as Teutonic quads . . .'

'Oh, of course,' replied the drummer, 'you had a Siamese twin wrapped round your neck and were trying to sell us some ointment to cure paranoia. Bugger off now, or we'll get nasty.'

Against all reason, Reuben went on to tell them

about the 'magic token' they'd promised him and which had actually arrived in his private parts. To prove it he took out the tin. Before he could open it the four women denied everything.

'We don't promise to send tins to anyone's private parts.'

Reuben was close to despair. 'But the blond hair . . .'

The lead guitarist asked her cousin what she thought she was doing bringing along a dickhead like this before the performance. The bass and the rhythm guitarist called their personal bodyguard. Reuben was grabbed and chucked out of the dressing-room, and all the vociferous protestations of a man whose rights have been violated had no effect whatsoever.

The bikers' leader had great difficulty justifying herself to her cousin and her fellow musicians.

'He was beaten up by a vicar this afternoon and they say his parents have killed themselves,' she said, after Reuben had been removed. 'Perhaps that's unbalanced him mentally.'

She was interrupted by the Flesh-eating Fetish Bitches' manager. Waving her bamboo stick around and emitting enormous clouds of cigar smoke, she announced she had just had a brilliant idea. The band should change its image and appear as blond quadruplets from now on. All their protests were in vain. The new dress regulations came in with immediate effect. A local shop specialising in false hair was rung up and told to bring four identical, long blond wigs before the concert started.

After the incident in the musicians' dressing-room, Reuben inclined more and more to the view that the four pallid females at the petrol-station must have been impostors, though impostors with remarkable 'magical' talents, as the mysterious appearance of the hair demonstrated. Was someone playing games with him?

He wondered whether he felt like going to the concert at all now. Eventually he decided he would stay and use his complimentary ticket. It turned out to be genuine, which made the whole affair even more confusing.

He was careful to avoid meeting the bikers, especially their leader, again. He also wanted to make sure, after everything that had happened, that the musicians wouldn't recognise him among the audience. He chose a seat as far away from the stage as possible. The lights went out. Immediately the audience struck up the traditional chant of, 'Who can say where the lights go when they go out?'

A Gustav Meyrink impersonator came on. In expressionist tones he announced the warm-up group, The Swinnskjöll Family. The response was whistles and catcalls. The stage was crammed full of utensils and appliances, as if for a live episode of a soap opera. From right to left there were: a front door with sound-box, a path laid with concrete slabs, a garden gate in a rustic fence complete with posts, an electric workbench, a chain saw, a hammer drill, a lot of planks and beams, a motorbike, two cars. Supported by a police guard, The Swinnskjöll Family came on: grandfather, father, mother, daughter, son as well as three adolescent boys, presumably friends of the son.

Father Swinnskjöll positioned himself at the microphone, gabbling gibberish without rhyme or reason. He accused the audience of having published some newspaper article or other about him, adding that enough was enough. A full beer-can hit him on the gob, there were cries of 'Yeuch' and 'Get off'. Then one of the policemen drew his gun and stepped to the front of the stage.

'Let the man have his say,' he shouted.

This produced even louder expressions of displeasure. Swinnskjöll swore and said he was going to give up appearing on stage. He had it all in black and white, but if that's what people wanted, then let them 'go down that road'. And anyway, he had his doubts whether 'that lot down there' paid their taxes like decent people. The extremely vulgar shouts increased and again beer-cans were thrown at him. The policeman shot into the crowd, though only with blanks, thank God. He was laughed off the stage. The Gustav Meyrink impersonator returned.

'A big hand for The Swinnskjöll Family,' he demanded.

A well-aimed can knocked the Gustav Meyrink out of him. In his place a policeman in a safety helmet took over the emceeing.

'And now a composition by Mother Swinnskjöll entitled, 'The Security Light Stays'. Give them a big hand.'

There was no applause, though plenty of oral imitations of noises from the digestive tract. Grandfather Swinnskjöll, a scrawny ghost in a track-suit, stood right at the edge of the stage emitting sounds which recalled a muezzin going both deaf and mad whilst carrying out his duties. For a while the son banged the front door shut in time to the music. In a neat switch, one of the policemen took over this activity so that Son Swinnskjöll could perform a step-dance in his army boots on the concrete slabs. Mother and daughter accompanied with high-pitched screeches. Father Swinnskjöll, still annoyed with the audience, spat with feeling onto the stage. Meanwhile his son had turned his attention to the garden gate. He flung it open and slammed it shut again and again with such force that as one man the audience leapt back a few yards. The explosive crash of the garden gate combined in a most sophisticated manner with the banging of the front door. Now the daughter was in one of the cars and kept on starting up the engine, which stalled every time, creating very unconventional syncopations. Father Swinnskjöll set the second car going, producing a heavy diesel ostinato. Mother Swinnskjöll began pounding on the concrete slabs with a spade in unison with her screeches. That was the signal for the son's three friends to start bellowing like animals. The father quickly cut a few dozen planks and beams to length and then nailed them together into a ramshackle hut in which the boys rode up the walls on bar-stools, braying all the time. The son-and-heir managed to start his motorbike and harmonise it with the two cars, without interrupting his perform-ance on the garden gate. On top of this continuo, the father improvised on workbench and chain-saw, even adding some telling flourishes with the hammer drill.

The whole time the audience were trying to shout down the noise, but there was no point. No one had any cans left to throw, so they had to use seats and bricks instead. Even a small woman was chucked at the Swinnskjölls. She knocked the grandfather over. His son abandoned his infernal machines and rushed to the front of the stage. Red as a lobster and snarling with rage, he swore at the audience and gave them the finger. This gesture brought a different police unit onto the scene who were at loggerheads with the band's police guard. They managed to club Father Swinnskjöll to the ground with their truncheons just in time before he could saw the small woman in two. His brazen denial of having made the aforementioned gesture got him nowhere. All this made the band's police guard jealous, and they forgot they were supposed to be protecting the Swinnskjöll Family. Soon, from force of habit, all the officers were laying into the heavy industrial band and their machines. Finally there was peace and quiet. The police withdrew en masse. The organiser came to the microphone with a correction.

'The composition you have just heard was erroneously announced as 'The Security Light Stays' whereas in fact it was a number entitled 'It's very early, people are still sleeping'. We hope you will excuse our mistake.'

Once the stage had been cleared and disinfected the concert could go on.

'Ladies and gentlemen, the Flesh-eating Fetish Bitches!'

The proverbial thunder of applause filled the concert hall. After what they had just been through, the people were simply happy and grateful to be able to applaud again. Clouds of smoke and mist rose up in a flicker of multicoloured lights. Four figures came onto the stage. Reuben started in surprise. From where he was sitting he couldn't see them in detail (given the lighting, even those right at the front probably couldn't either) but they definitely had long blond hair and were uniform in appearance. From close up it was possible – just – to see that they were unclothed and covered from head to toe in a thick crust of mud. Reuben, of course, knew nothing of their manager's brain-wave and so wondered whether he was going out of his mind. To reassure himself, he asked some of those sitting around him whether they too saw four blonde look-alikes on the stage. They all confirmed they did. Then he was overwhelmed by the sudden, brutal onslaught of music being pumped out of a thousand speakers. Like a puppet on a string in the grip of the beat, he jigged about in the aisle and screamed himself hoarse. Two hours later one of the cleaners spoke to him. 'You can stop now, it's all finished.'

Reuben came to. The lights in the concert hall were on, the audience had left, the stage was empty.

'They all went home ages ago,' said the cleaner.

His behaviour had convinced her she was confronted with one of those wretched glue-sniffers, if not worse. She knew from experience that philo-

sophical niceties were wasted on them. But the
vigorous application of a sopping floorcloth was
certainly capable of establishing an isomorphism
between two brains, however differently they might
function. If necessary, the long handle of the scrub-
bing brush could be broken off and employed as an
extra deterrent. Reuben, who was nowhere near as
mad as she assumed, felt ashamed and beat a hasty
retreat.

There were four blondes playing on the stage, that
had been confirmed by several others in the audience.
Of course, those people could just as well have been
part of an hallucination, or of a conspiracy against
him. If things went on like this, *he* would be the one
needing an ointment to cure paranoia. Now what had
made him think of that? Where had he heard of
it before? Oh yes, the drummer of the Flesh-eating
Fetish Bitches had mentioned such an ointment. In
the dressing-room, where the four of them had not
been the least bit blonde and had vehemently denied
ever having been so. And yet shortly afterwards, on
stage, they had been . . . Reuben desperately needed
to get things sorted out in his mind. When had all
this started? When he went to the petrol-station to
buy opaque white. Was there perhaps some connection? An opaque white ointment for paranoia? (Both
white, squashy and available in tubes?)

You may well be wondering what a seventeen-
year-old, who could at best be credited with adolescent insecurity, would know about paranoia? In
this particular case, however, one must bear in mind
that Reuben Hecht had already been seventeen for

twenty years and had thus had the opportunity to acquire a familiarity with paranoia corresponding roughly to that of a thirty-seven-year-old. He could well appreciate that the whole universe existed solely for the purpose of driving him to the wall, or up it. A genuine thirty-seven-year-old would have realised the utter hopelessness of defying such superior forces and given way to resignation. Not so a seventeen-year-old, however long he had been seventeen. The natural irrationality and rebelliousness of that age, tempered in this particular case by twenty years of exposure to the world, stifled all impulse meekly to submit to any kind of *force majeure*.

Determined to tear apart the web of delusion that was being spun round him, Reuben resolved to begin by analysing the underlying pattern of events. However, the cleaner had shooed him out of the building and once outside other questions took precedence over his web-pattern analysis. It was dark, but how late was it? The dial of his watch was black: new moon. But up in the sky was a full moon and the dial of the moon said seventeen minutes past eleven.

'Hey!?' exclaimed Reuben indignantly. He shook his head and everything was back in order again. The moon (it was indeed a new moon) was obviously fast, since his wrist watch said only eight minutes past eleven. He had to phone home. There was a telephone box opposite the concert hall. Hardly had he taken a few steps towards it than a vehicle came up from behind and slowly drove past him, tooting its horn. It was a white minibus, *the* white minibus with the pallid Teutonic maidens from the petrol station looking out of the windows. It was them, there was no doubt about it. The driver wound down her window.

'Hi there!' she shouted. 'How did you like the concert?'

The surprise triggered off a slight hebephrenic-paranoid trauma in Reuben (similar to hiccoughs only psychological). What he actually thought was, 'She's wound down her *wig low*,' which produced a completely different, distorted, not to say absurd image. He stood there at the kerb, clasping his arms round himself tight, so as not to fall apart laughing. Fortunately the trauma passed quickly. Of sound mind once more, though completely exhausted, he shouted back,

'Wonderful! Out of this world! But why did you disclaim all knowledge of me in your dressing-room? And what about your hair? It was red or black in there, but when you appeared on stage it was the same as it is now? Oh, and by the way, your magic token arrived.' He patted the relevant part of his jacket.[1]

'Great! Keep it up!' said the driver. 'But if you'll excuse us now, we have to get on.' With that she

---

[1] It is a matter of demonstrable fact that two great contemporary authors, Gronius and Rauschenbach, would have formulated this as follows: 'He thwacked his leather jerkin.' (Huflattich, Stümper & ff Editions no. 6: 'Ausflug à l'pinesque oder Fleisch und Kohlen aus Rixdorf'; also in: *Stücke 1*, Edition echoraum, Vienna, 1993, p. 64; English translation: '*Expédition à l'pinesque* or Flesh and Coals from Sawtry', Barringlane Books, Peterborough, 2001.)

wound up the window and the minibus disappeared into the distance.

'What was all that about?' Reuben shouted. 'Why can't I ever get a straight answer from you? I'm starting to get sick and tired of all this mystification! What is it about me that makes everyone treat me like this?'

Furious, he stomped over to the telephone box. All he needed now was for his parents to be really dead and for him to get put in the children's home. Might not Harprecht and Herkenrath appear out of the darkness at any moment and fall on him? The telephone was an old one that took coins and actually worked. And Reuben had the right coins! He could even remember his parents' number and there were no complications with dialling. But nobody answered. He had decided he would wait for an hour and try three more times, so he stuck it out in the telephone box and dialled every twenty minutes. Each time all he could hear was the ringing tone. Why couldn't something bizarre but nice happen to him, just for once? Was it that fate was too stupid, or did it really have it in for him? Usually when he made a phone call there was Godknowswho on the line, there had even been unintentional tripartite or quadripartite conversations. He willed something like that to happen for his fourth and final try. Over the monotonously pulsating buzz, signalling that he should now put his declared intention of starting a new life into operation, he wanted to hear the loud and clear voices of two women. One ought to say,

'There's a ringing tone suddenly started on the line.'

'*And I can hear someone breathing,*' the other should reply.

'*Hey, you,*' the first one ought to snap, '*either say something or put the bloody receiver down.*'

Reuben's first thought would be, '*That can't be the Flesh-eating Fetish Bitches again, can it?*'

In spite of that, he would explain who he was and the situation he was in.

One of the women on the line would take pity on him.

'*Oh you poor thing! To have to start a new life in the middle of the night with no idea where . . . Tell me where you are. I'll come and fetch you.*'

Not even the emphatic warning from the other woman would stop her. Reuben was already imagining the happy life to which he would be transported through this stroke of good fortune: never having to do another drawing, being pampered by the charming young woman, possibly even winning a substantial sum on the lottery . . .

Reuben inserted his coins once more, dialled and concentrated. Two voices, over the background of the ringing tone, were indeed to be heard.

'There's a ringing tone suddenly started on the line,' said one.

'And I can hear someone breathing,' said the other.

'Hey, you! Say something or put the bloody receiver down,' the first voice snapped.

Reuben needed no further invitation. 'My name is Reuben Hecht,' he said. 'I have to start a new life and it's the middle of the night. I'm in the telephone box opposite the concert hall. Can you pick me up?'

'Reuben Hecht!' chorused the two voices, suddenly sounding very familiar.

'Stay where you are,' said the one.

'We're on our way,' said the other.

Reuben realised then that it was Harprecht and Herkenrath. Of all people! Fate must have gone completely doolally. He dashed out of the telephone box. He had to get away from there as quickly as possible! Reuben ran across the road, disappeared down a side street, twisted and turned, ran up alleys at random and then out again. It didn't take him back to the place he started out from, but it did take him to a place where he had absolutely no idea where he was. Most parts of the town were unknown to him, including this one. That didn't really matter, though, since he was going to start a new life anyway. He might just as well travel to a different town. He got on the first bus to appear. Two marks eighty would take him to the edge of the town, where there should be a connecting bus to one of the neighbouring towns. When he arrived at the terminus, Reuben discovered that there was indeed a late bus on which he could get to the big city twenty kilometres away. He was the only passenger and during the whole journey the single driver (there was no guessing game) left him in peace. Twenty minutes later they had reached the city terminus, a bus station called 'Holzhindenburg'. There was no chance of going any farther that night.

It was getting on for half past two. Reuben was dog-tired. He urgently needed to find somewhere to spend the night. Since he was under-age and almost penniless, a bed in an hotel was out of the question. But he had to get off the street at all costs to avoid being picked up by the police. The situation was starting to look as bad as all those years ago on the Ivory Coast. And there he'd at least had the exile address of the Holy German Paintbrush Distance Learning Academy Defectors, even if he didn't actually get there. He would have given a lot for an address like that in his present predicament. To find out whether there was a branch of the Distance Learning Academy Defectors somewhere in the city, he went to the telephone box next to the bus-station. The phone book, which he intended to consult, had been removed by some strong-arm vandal, along with the receiver. There was no other telephone box to be seen anywhere around. He'd just have to set off at random until he found one.

The district was pretty run-down. Roughly every third house was empty and for shops the figure was every second. The walls were covered with the usual sameness of aerosol excreta. The pavements were strewn with devastating amounts of rubbish. The street lighting was defective. Nowhere was anyone to be seen or heard, which, under the present circumstances, was more of a comfort than anything else. The police surely wouldn't risk coming to an area like this, or would find it too nauseating. It suddenly occurred to Reuben that there might be large, ferocious dogs roaming the empty streets. Hardly had the idea entered his head than he heard a distant wolf-like howling. He thought of his bed at home and of the pyjamas he still had from the moonlanding.

How far beyond his reach they were now! For all the vexations of life at home, his parents' house had at least given him the security of a fixed abode. Only the memory of the torment twenty years of drawing had caused him, prevented Reuben from seeing that security in an idealised rosy glow. If his parents should happen still to be alive, then the price for sleeping in his old bed again would be a dear one indeed: the resumption of the degrading course of study in official illustration. And if they really were dead, then all he could look forward to was a bed in the dormitory of the children's home where Harprecht and Herkenrath wanted to incarcerate him. He just had to pull himself together and continue on his way, even though it took him past derelict buildings and outrageous piles of rubbish, always expecting the worst and almost falling apart from exhaustion and hunger.

It had grown visibly darker. Clearly he had crossed some Rubicon beyond which the street lighting did not work at all. As far as he could see, before him lay a pitch-dark — Lovecraft would have written 'blasphemous' — defile between looming buildings. In contrast to his home town, the full moon was not shining here. A thin sickle was all that could be seen in the sky. And nowhere a telephone box. 'The best thing would be to be dead,' thought Reuben. His drooping head and sagging legs, above all his turned-in toes and buttocks clenched with fear, gave physical expression to his mood. He felt like a wooden figure crudely put together out of separate parts or, even more, like bones in an old grave. His further thoughts were, 'Well, here I am, big head, short legs. The distance from the curve of my buttocks to my feet is just about a quarter of the whole.'

His impression of his own anatomy was a result of his horror at the situation he found himself in. His exhaustion was turning into a feverish condition.

Ex-medical officer of health Rossman stepped out of the darkness to examine him. His diagnosis was, 'Poverty of form, as in an unassuming animal.' He poked and prodded Reuben with his cold fingers and metal snow-shovel. Like a police pathologist conducting an autopsy, he dictated his observations into a small microphone, 'No attempt at all to be true to life. Patient not in possession of clearly defined extremities, would probably like to be construed as a Christ-child. The only thing about him the presence of which can be unequivocally established is his gigantic nose. The rest is a tangle of curves not amenable to more precise determination.'

Suddenly there were a number of reporters there, excitedly asking the doctor layman's questions:

'Doesn't this call for a vaginal examination?'

'Could you give us some information about your activities?'

With a pompous gesture, the doctor refused to answer. Using a mirror and a magnifying glass, he had made further observations:

'Low thorax with no characteristics of a broad, conical female breast. At the lower lip of the wooden trunk the arms begin with props or tendons. What at first sight appears to be a belly with flaccid tissue is in fact a lung. Useless as an internal organ, consequently attached externally. Not a rationally ordered, realistic human being.'

Plagued by countless abnormal bodily sensations, Reuben dragged himself along. Rossman just kept on talking, his Red-Cross cap bracing itself against the night sky. The two reporters turned into Prümers, the parish priest, boasting of having crucified Christ. He commanded Reuben to reflect on the mortal sin he had committed in his behaviour towards his parents.

'We'll put the Angel of Death onto you!' he yelled.

'And the Insanity Commissioners!' added Rossman.

Reuben wasn't listening. Looking down a side street, he saw a faint gleam some fifty metres away. The light from a telephone box!

'Oh, that's a pub frequented by cannibals,' said Rossman. 'Go on in, you'll have a knife sticking in you in no time at all.'

'It's enough to make me laugh myself silly!' exclaimed Prümers. 'Perhaps Christ's even in there, waiting to crucify you!'

Reuben made his way to the telephone box as quickly as he could. It was one of the old yellow ones, not one of those poncy affairs in white, grey and pink. He hoped against hope that the appliance would be in working order despite the character of the district. He didn't give three-quarters of a pound of precocious sausage for the delirious ranting of Rossman and Prümers. He went into the telephone box. Miraculously, neither the telephone book nor the apparatus had been damaged. Unfortunately, however many times he thumbed through the fat tome, he could not find an entry under 'Holy German Paintbrush Distance Learning Academy Defectors'. Nor was there anything under 'exile'. He made one last attempt and looked up 'Distance Learning Academy'. As he was flicking through, what should happen to catch his eye but the 'Flesh-eating Fetish Bitches' Fan Club'!

'Now there's a thing!' muttered Reuben in amazement.

Since, as he quickly ascertained, there was no entry under 'Distance Learning Academy', he inserted his coins and on the spur of the moment dialled the number of the fan club. He did not feel the late hour would be a problem. Anyone who was an organised supporter of a group like that would definitely not be asleep yet. And this assessment of the situation turned out to be right. The receiver was lifted and a cheerfully tipsy female voice answered. Reuben told her, and it was nothing but the truth, that he had just attended the Flesh-eating Fetish Bitches' concert in his home town, was a complete stranger in the city, had had all kinds of experiences with the band and, lacking the most basic necessities, was appealing to the solidarity of a fellow fan.

'Wow, baby, you're singin' my song,' said the fan-club woman. 'No sweat, I'll come an' pick you up. Where are you at the moment?'

Reuben told her what was written on the dial of the telephone.

'Heeyyy, just you hold on a minute now,' the

71

woman replied, 'I'm not driving down there. Even the police don't risk going to that district.'

So she gave him an involved description of where she would meet him and how to get there. The combination of her drunkenness and his exhaustion made communication difficult. Reuben couldn't quite follow what she was saying, but didn't like to keep on asking her to repeat things, as he didn't want to irritate her, nor to sound like a complete prat. The result was that he had no idea of the way. Nevertheless, he told her he'd got it. She promised to be there as quickly as possible and hung up. Reuben thought hard. 'First go along the side street to the end,' that he could remember. Then what? Up some wall or other?

Rossman was squawking in his ear, 'Off you go to your Miss Pussywhipper, then. She'll make you into her sex-slave, hook you up to corpses and ice, and keep you jiggling on an electrical circuit for weeks on end!'

Not to be left out, Prümers added, 'They're already lying in wait for you at her house. They'll bury you alive in the cellar!'

Reuben wandered round the streets at random. He no longer had any idea what the rendezvous point was. A church? The square outside the opera? The zoo? He was too tired to think. Two streets further on he came to a large square covered with the tents, booths and caravans of a freak show. Above it, in megalomaniac neon letters, was written:

THE
100,000-ELECTRIC-RAYS-FROM-HEAVEN
REVELATION OF THE
WONDERS OF THE WORLD

In classic American freak-show manner, gigantic posters enticed the public with crudely sensationalist portrayals of the attractions inside the booths and tents. For a while Reuben stood at the entrance looking at the posters. Prümers poured his vitriol over the 'terrible blasphemy' of the pictures while Rossman played the art critic: 'No one can deny that these pictorial representations are worse than anything currently to be seen and thoroughly deserve the designation 'inferior art'. They manage, with a distorting intensity, to combine the deformities of a hideous overall impression with insanely bizarre individual touches.'

At the sight of one poster Rossman fell into a rage. According to the text it represented:

THE ELECTRICAL ARCHQUEEN FROM THE BLACK FOREST WITH HER CROWN OF MARBLE WHO, BY MEANS OF THE MYSTERIOUS POWERS OF HER SEXUAL ORGANS, CAN MAKE BULBS SCREWED INTO THEM SHINE WITH A BRILLIANT LIGHT AND CAN TRANSFER THE MOST UNHEARD-OF MUSIC DIRECTLY FROM HER HEAD ONTO DISC. PRICE PER RECORD: DM 39.90

'No talent, no flair at all!' screamed Rossman. 'The

treatment of the lower section is particularly revolting and is in embarrassing contrast to the way the upper part has been dealt with. And then the crude, street-urchin style in which the genitals have been drawn . . .'

Prümers interrupted him. 'Come on, quick. I've discovered there's a church just round the corner where the faithful are whipped with garden hoses every Sunday.'

With that, his two tormentors were gone and Reuben could examine the garish posters in peace. They did seem to be fundamentally unartistic, though the only thing that bothered him about them was that they reminded him of his illustration course. All he wanted to do was to sleep, just sleep. Suddenly a small door opened somewhere in the freak show and the marble-crowned Archqueen from the Black Forest came out.

'Were we speaking on the telephone?' she asked Reuben.

Confused, he replied, 'I was speaking to a young lady on the phone just now, but I had no idea that you –'

'That's OK,' the Archqueen broke in, indicating that he should follow her.

Reuben could not believe she was the drunken female who had made the rendezvous with him. The Archqueen was completely sober. She was an imposing figure of a woman with red hair and wearing a long-sleeved leotard of artificial leopard skin. Her feet had been painted blue. Given the way she looked, though, the idea that she was the woman he had been talking to seemed not entirely unreasonable. But hadn't she been going to pick him up in her car somewhere?

'A bit odd for the fan club to have its office in a freak show,' he thought. 'But it doesn't bother me. Just as long as I'm off the streets and can get some shut-eye.'

The woman led him between several booths and tents to a grandiose caravan in a rather indeterminate architectural style. No security light went on as the two approached. Reuben saw there was a carved inscription over the door:

DELAWARE VILLA

Not a word about the Flesh-eating Fetish Bitches' fan club. No brass plate, not even a chalk scribble. The marble-crowned electric Archqueen opened the door. In the gloom Reuben followed her through an entrance hall furnished in a fussy, aggravated Victorian style. The dark brown Flemish staircase they came to was made from the wood of colour-blind trees usually reserved for the manufacture of cocktail sticks.

Going up, Reuben examined the paintings on the walls of the staircase, as far as the pale gleam of the alabaster hanging lamps allowed. Pictures again! Up to the first floor they were portraits of the most famous Delaware chiefs, including among others Aromance, Sweetmilk, Dynamo and even one called Hecht! On the first floor they went along a corridor which ended in another staircase. The paintings there were unrecognisable, depicting as they did centennial examples of interference on vision. The guest-room was in the attic. Reuben was relieved when the woman showed no sign of wanting to make conversation or to compel him to spend the night listening to records. She just showed him the room, wished him good night and disappeared. Reuben bolted the door. Without excessive washing at the hand-basin, he undressed down to his underwear, which was, thank God, free of oil-paint, got into bed and immediately fell asleep.

At about eight o'clock in the morning the freaks all around came to noisy life. As he woke up too, Reuben, who disliked being reminded of his existence, again thought, 'And I'm going to have to die some day as well.'

This was the day his new life was supposed to start in earnest. He was horribly hungry and set off in search of the kitchen. He found it on the ground floor. The Archqueen was there already, making breakfast. She had a ghostly look as she moved about in the glow of the fire. From above, pale light came in through the smoke-hole. Reuben was going to wish her a polite 'Good morning' when a loud-speaker suddenly gave out a crude and disgustingly primitive, 'Ai-ya-yakka-berwakka.'

'Whatever's that?' he cried out in alarm.

'Music from the Colony,' the woman replied. 'By the aboriginals.'

The Archqueen looked as if she was more suited to a night club than an early-morning kitchen. Nevertheless she was expert at making breakfast.

'But there aren't any recordings of the music of the aboriginals from the Colony,' objected Reuben.

The Archqueen proudly pointed to a cassette recorder and said, 'There are here.'

Reuben had heard or read various reports that so far there had been no research into the aboriginals' music, nor even any recordings of it. It was so alien that no one could listen to it.

'Where did these recordings come from?' he asked. Had the woman been to the Colony? he wondered. Had she braved all sorts of dangers and adventures to make some unique recordings?

'No, I haven't been to the Colony. I can receive the aboriginals' music and record it onto tape, like recording from the radio.'

'What do you use to receive it?'

'A piece of wire in my head.'

'Did you have it inserted specifically for that?'

'Don't be silly. Actually, it's all the result of a mistake. My father was a very keen amateur physiologist, specialising in the brain. He was always trying things out on me when I was a child. Sometimes, when we had visitors or my parents were a bit bored, he used to lay me down on the table and sticks bits of wire into specific parts of my head.'

Reuben was horrified. She had to calm him down.

'I was given a local anaesthetic, of course. The brain itself is impervious to pain. My father passed a weak current through the wires, triggering off different reactions in me. At the press of a button I would, for example, eat, drink or carry out various tasks of personal hygiene. Once my father stimulated a part of my cerebellum that he would have done better to have left unstimulated. My hair stood on end, I craned my neck, gave loud cries of alarm and panicked. Screeching with terror, I rose up into the air and fluttered away from the table, at the same time pulling all the wires out. One broke off, leaving a piece stuck in my head. It didn't trouble me, so we left it in there. But from that day on I could hear this strange music every time my head was inclined at a particular angle. Only in mono, unfortunately.'

She inclined her head to give Reuben a brief demonstration of the required position. Then she went on,

'For a long time I had no idea what I was hearing. At first I didn't even know it was music. Many years later I happened by chance to come into possession of a few aboriginal records. They were rather thick and cold, like frozen potato cakes. In order to be able to play them I had to construct a suitable gramophone. It was only then that I realised the music on the records was same as I received with the broken-off wire in my head.'

Reuben would, he said, be fascinated to hear how she managed to record the music in her head onto tape.

'I have a special cable I can use to tap directly into the wire. Otherwise I'd have to have a neuro-socket fixed in the back of my neck.'

'But where do you think this music comes from?' Reuben asked. 'Could it be an aboriginal transmitter?'

'No idea. Perhaps I'll never know. How should I?'

Then Reuben remembered something he'd read the previous night on the poster.

'Aha, so that's the music you transfer directly from your head onto disc?'

'Yes.'

'So there are recordings of aboriginal music you can buy after all.'

The Archqueen shook her head. 'Not one disc has been produced yet. The man who's supposed to be organising the technical side hasn't done a thing so far.'

'Sounds very organised.'

'He claimed he'd done all the groundwork and it was going to be a *superb* edition with one of the very *top* record companies. Since then we've been waiting a whole year and nothing at all has happened.'

In an outburst of youthful impetuosity Reuben exclaimed, 'That's no use! You should avoid any business dealings with people like that! Would you like me to arrange it for you?'

He surprised himself with his outspokenness.

'Eat your breakfast first,' said the electric Archqueen. 'The manager would like to see you as soon as possible.'

Reuben felt alarmed, but his instinct told him it would be better not to show it. Outwardly he remained calm and unconcerned. The manager? He wondered why the manager would want to speak to *him*. Still nothing had been said about the fan club, and he wasn't going to be the one to start. It could be they thought he was someone else. Mistaken identity

79

was in at the moment, and popular with writers as well (but one shouldn't overdo it).

The Archqueen sat down at the table to have her breakfast with Reuben. It was then he saw that she was not, as he had assumed, wearing a short-sleeved T-shirt and a skirt over her leopard-skin leotard. Her arms and legs were bare, but still had the same pattern as the leotard.

It was indiscreet, but he still asked, 'Are those tattoos?'

'No. Just one of the vagaries of nature. Patches of pigmentation. Like other people's freckles, only in my case for a change they're set out in a leopard-skin pattern. It's like that all over my body.'

Reuben was amazed. 'Wow, that's fantastic! The wire *and* the genuine leopard skin! You really are one of the main attractions of the show!'

He remembered something else from the poster. 'And how do you make bulbs light up with your sexual organs?'

Most of all he would have liked to ask her for a demonstration there and then (which would also have permitted him to see more of her skin patterning), but he restrained himself.

'That's my little secret. I'm something special, you see.'

In order to stop the conversation getting round to himself, Reuben immediately enquired about something else. He was interested to know where the name 'Delaware Villa' came from. The explanation he was given was as follows:

'The liquidation of the bankrupt Delaware estate

provided the raw materials for the schnapps factory which the manager, whom you will meet in a few minutes, set up in 1890. It was so flourishing he became immortal and was even in a position to open the '100,000-Electric-Rays-from-Heaven-Revelation of the Wonders of the World'. In memory of the Delawares, to whom in a way he owed everything, he named his own home after them.'

'Oh yes, the Delawares,' mused Reuben. 'They had such beautiful songs and dances and existed . . .'

'Until they ran out of time and had to call in the receivers,' said the leopard-skin lady.

When they had finished breakfast, they got up.

'Come along, Herr Sondergeld,' she said, 'the manager's waiting.'

Once more Reuben made every effort to keep his expression blank. Who was Sondergeld? What was expected of him? And why didn't he just clear up the misunderstanding?

She took him into a narrow, high room. The walls groaned under the weight of tapestries (depicting scenes from the life of hairdressers), done by high-warp weaving. Spread around the room were a number of unknown instruments and two mechanical adding machines. Reuben's attention was attracted to a framed drawing of shockingly poor quality propped up against the wall. There must be someone, somewhere, who was considerably worse at drawing than he was! Without thinking, he squatted down on his haunches and stared at it. If he had been asked to describe it he wouldn't have found it possible. Rossman might perhaps have been able to . . .

Everything about the drawing was outrageous, provoking comments of the type H. P. Lovecraft formulates in such a charmingly inflationary manner in his stories. The treatment of composition, anatomy, perspective, light and shade was truly scandalous. What the 'artist' had done with faces and parts of the body (especially with regard to the joints) *was* an 'unholy abomination'. No less deplorable was the technique employed. It was a complete mystery to Reuben, who, after twenty years in the graphic treadmill, still didn't know much about these matters, what had been used to produce such ink-marks on the paper. They hadn't been drawn with a pen, even he could tell that. He had a suspicion a ballpoint might have been involved. But would *anyone* let themselves be tempted into committing such an atrocity. For the sake of the creator's artistic soul, he hoped it was a Rapidograph, an instrument with a rigid point used with Indian ink in technical drawing. The cross-hatching could only be described as bestial. On the one hand arthritic scratching and scrawling, on the other the sheet had been covered in lines drawn with a ruler in an attempt to reproduce the style of a copper engraving. Was such a thing even *allowed*? Reuben imagined what would have happened to him if he had sent something like that in to the Holy German Paintbrush Distance Learning Academy.

'Is the name of the artist known?' he asked, appalled.

The leopard-woman seemed to think this some kind of joke. At least she laughed out loud as she said that young Herr Sondergeld certainly had a sense of humour, she had to grant him that. Reuben was just going to ask her what had made her laugh when the wall to his left opened up from ceiling to floor. It was an unusually high concealed door cunningly inserted into the wall; until that moment there had been nothing to indicate its presence. Panting and wheezing, a fat man of middle height and about sixty years of age came through the opening. His round head was completely bald and he had a cigar stuck in the corner of his mouth. He was wearing a white, open-necked shirt with the sleeves rolled up. His grey trousers had shiny patches and were held up with braces.[2]

'I've already had it framed,' he blared, pointing at the picture. 'I just don't know what to say. Indistinguishable from a genuine Buckauer! Impeccable!'

He shook Reuben firmly by the hand. 'Allow me to introduce myself: Scherer-Dextry, manager here. So this is what you look like, my dear Sondergeld. I have to say I imagined you a bit older, what?'

'Oh,' Reuben stammered, having no idea at all what to say, 'I . . . er . . . my glands . . .'

'Spare me the self-pity,' cried Scherer-Dextry, bursting into a fit of uncontrollable laughter.

The leopard-woman was leaning against the wall with an absent look on her face. She was holding her head inclined at the aforementioned angle. When he noticed this, the manager said, 'She's listening to

[2] So now you know what he looked like.

83

that dreadful music again. Come along, Sondergeld, we have to discuss your work.'

Incapable of pointing out what was obviously a case of mistaken identity, Reuben followed him through the concealed door and into his office. It was fairly dark and more or less as you would imagine a freak-show manager's office. From the ceiling hung the obligatory stuffed crocodile and on the tall shelves round the walls were countless freaks, freaks preserved in alcohol or formaldehyde or embalmed.

Scherer-Dextry beamed with pride. 'My own little chamber of wonders,' he said. Reuben peered apprehensively at some of the jars containing all sorts of monstrosities: various kinds of Siamese twins, four-legged birds, embryos with unorthodox heads, dugongs and God knows what else.

'Right,' said the manager, filling two glasses with rum, 'as we agreed in our correspondence, you can start at once. I can't wait to see how your Buckauer-style posters will turn out. The sample you sent is extremely promising. I'm very keen for you get down to work as soon as possible. That's why I summoned you in the middle of the night. Cheers.'

If Reuben hadn't been seventeen for twenty years now, he would not have been able to get the rum down. As it was, he was surprised how good it tasted. He took in less and less of what the manager was telling him, but enjoyed the rum. Would marzipan go with it? he wondered. Tears welled up in Scherer-Dextry's eyes. He knelt down before Reuben, dashing down one glass after the other.

'Listen, Sondergeld. There is a secret sorrow that

has for years been gnawing at my heart. I possess a good dozen Buckauer prints, and now your masterly copy to go with them, but it pains me more than I can say not to have any idea who Buckauer was – or is. You can't even tell from the signature whether it's a woman or a man. We must find out. The truth must be revealed! Buckauer's identity shall not remain a secret any longer! There must be research, long-overdue, systematic research into Buckauer. Every means must be employed, from the motor vehicle to the microwave cooker. I can't undertake this myself, I've a freak show to run. But a man like you, Sondergeld, a man like you could do it, I just know you could. It's a somewhat unusual penchant, I admit, but I'm sure you can understand? Tell me you understand. Please.'

'Oh I do,' replied Reuben, emboldened by the rum, 'I think it's entirely appropriate for the manager of a freak show –'

'God bless you, Sondergeld! You're the man for me! Before you start on the posters –'

Reuben pricked up his ears. *He* was supposed to design some posters? But Scherer-Dextry was already going on.

'– do some research into Buckauer. It's long overdue, and you'd be doing me a great favour.'

'I'll do anything,' Reuben thought, 'as long as I don't have to draw or paint,' and gave a nod of acquiescence. Scherer-Dextry kissed him on the forehead.

'Sondergeld! If you do that as well as you copied Buckauer's style I'll make you sole heir to my estate.

You must set off right away and check the telephone directories of every town and region. You'll also have to go through the personnel files of the army, the merchant navy and the voluntary fire brigades. Sift through police records, newspaper archives, death registers. All expenses paid, of course. Start this minute, so that the posters don't have to wait too long to get done. I'm relying on you.'

'This very day?' Reuben asked. 'It's Sunday.'

'I'll give you *this very Sunday*! When I say *this minute*, I mean *this minute*. And no arguing.'

With that he pushed Reuben out of the office and the concealed door closed without leaving the slightest chink. The leopard-woman was still standing in the same position, immersed in her music. Against the wall across the room from her was the blasted picture. Whatever Reuben's new situation was, one thing was certain: he had left painting and drawing behind him for good. Suddenly the woman came to.

'Finished already?' she asked.

'Yes,' said Reuben. 'I'm to set off this minute and find out everything about Buckauer.'

Even as he said that, he realised he had not the least desire to do it. He would rather stay with the leopard-woman. At her next public performance he intended to have a good look at the trick with the light-bulb.

'I can't do what the manager's asking of me,' he thought. 'How could I go sifting through police records? If the police see me they'll just keep me there. And then it'll be off to the children's home. There's only one thing for it: pretend to go on the research trip and start a new life somewhere else under a veil of secrecy.'

'Well then, have fun,' said the electric Archqueen. 'For my part I think I'll have a second breakfast. Listening to the music in my head always makes me hungry.'

Reuben was starting to get sleepy from the effects of the rum, so he decided to join the woman. As he went out, he threw one last contemptuous glance at Sondergeld's imitation Buckauer. At that moment the concealed door was flung open. His bald head as bright as a beetroot, Scherer-Dextry rushed out, shouting,

'Stop! Wait! Come back at once! New situation! Global delete!'

Reuben nearly jumped out of his skin. 'He's found out I'm not Sondergeld,' he thought. But that couldn't be the case, for Scherer-Dextry was already going on, 'Sondergeld, my dear Sondergeld. A further change in your assignment. Please forgive me, but this has absolute priority. I've just had a call from the Colony. Worldchild and Kneerider —'

'Huh, Worldchild and Kneerider, those two wallies,' said the Archqueen and went out, adding, 'I'm off to the kitchen.'

'Worldchild and Kneerider,' Scherer-Dextry continued, 'have just reported the appearance of androids derived from UHT milk. Just imagine, Sondergeld, androids from milk! I simply must have some for the 100,000-Electric-Rays-from-Heaven-Revelation of the Wonders of the World. Get some.'

'Me?'

'Yes, you. And whenever you have a window in your android-procurement programme, you carry on with your Buckauer research, understood? No swanning around. Of course, what I'd like best would be for you to come back with a few of these lactically engineered androids as well as some positive facts on Buckauer.'

Whatever next? Reuben just couldn't wait to get the hell out of there.

'Hold on a minute,' said Scherer-Dextry, 'you can't go to the Colony by yourself. You need some back-up. Edwina!'

Back-up? That meant someone keeping an eye on him. Reuben felt uneasy. How was he going to get out of this if he let himself get stuck with a minder?

'Edwina!' Scherer-Dextry shouted again.

The door, through which the leopard-woman had gone out, opened and a girl of about six entered the room. Even though she was a pretty, slightly oriental-looking girl, who in a dozen years or so might well turn into a more-than-presentable young woman, Reuben found it hard to see her as the promised back-up. Instead of getting stuck with a minder, it looked as if he'd been given someone *he* would have to keep an eye on.

Scherer-Dextry introduced them and explained the assignment. Reuben didn't want to seem impolite to the child, but at the first opportunity of a tête-à-tête with the manager he was going to ask him what he thought he was doing. When the task had been explained to Edwina, she looked at Reuben earnestly and said, 'We can set off straightaway. Please go to the kitchen and put some provisions together. I'll go and change quickly and collect my things.'

She spoke just like a grown-up, apart from her voice. 'Another of these precocious children,' thought Reuben. He loathed children anyway. There couldn't be anything worse than travelling round with a child. Hardly had Edwina left than he was furiously voicing his misgivings to the freak-show manager.

'I can't explain it,' Scherer-Dextry replied, 'but she's not only a little girl. But what's the point of me going on, you'll just have to wait and see. You go off to the kitchen now, Sondergeld, and put some provisions together. All the best!'

With that the fat man disappeared and the concealed door closed behind him again.

The best thing would be to do a runner right away, Reuben thought. He decided to slip past the kitchen and leave Delaware Villa and the whole freak-show site by the shortest route. Unfortunately nothing came of his plan. The leopard-woman was looking out for him.

'If you're going to the Colony, could you please take the opportunity of finding out where the music I receive through the wire in my head comes from?'

'Of course. Sure there's nothing else you'd like me to do?' asked Reuben sarcastically. He was pissed off because his escape plan had been thwarted. He wanted to scream out loud that he wasn't Sondergeld and that as far as he was concerned, they could all screw themselves all the way to the Colony and back. However, it seemed wiser not to make a scene, to

agree to everything then scarper as fast as possible.
But nothing came of this either. He heard steps
approaching. Edwina already? Had she changed that
quickly? She had indeed, she'd changed completely.
What came into the kitchen was a casually dressed,
fully developed woman in her mid-to-late twenties.
There was no doubt that it was the same Edwina, she
just looked as if she'd been away for a good twenty
years. But Reuben didn't cotton on to that. He really
thought a different woman had come in. The electric
Archqueen had to explain the awkward situation.

'Well blow me!' he exclaimed. 'Have twenty years
gone already?'

The two women calmly explained it to him again.
The reason for the transformation was that Edwina
lasted longer if she went round as a child.

'It's an energy-saving measure,' she said. 'I can't
afford to embody my true age, energy-wise. I'm
actually sixty-five, you see.'

It bore a distant similarity to Reuben's own
problem. 'I've been seventeen for the last twenty
years,' he blurted out, and immediately wondered
whether it had been wise to do so. He heard the
leopard-woman acknowledge that this was a plausible explanation for his youthful appearance. Scherer-
Dextry had commented on it as well.

Suddenly everything was different; that is, much
better. He was glad he hadn't just cleared off. He
would love to travel round with an attractive woman
like that.

'Then let's get those provisions sorted out,' he
cried excitedly. He made sure there were plenty of

sandwiches, and also a bottle of rum and some blocks of marzipan. Shortly after twelve Edwina and Reuben left Delaware Villa.

'Please remember to find out where the aboriginal music in my head comes from,' the Archqueen reminded him.

II

Together with their old personalities, which the furious bus-drivers had thrashed out of them, Harprecht and Herkenrath had lost the lives they had lived until then. Harprecht was no longer accepted as Rossman, the medical officer of health, and not just because his new name was spelt completely differently. More significant was the fact that he lacked both medical knowledge and any ambition in that direction. He now imagined he could earn a living completing psychological tests in magazines and sending the results in to the editors.

Herkenrath too was fully occupied sending material through the post. In his case it was letters with questions and suggestions for books, which he sent to a publisher. He was convinced he was a nature writer; above all he felt he had a contribution to make to the education of young people. Since he was no longer Prümers the parish priest, his former congregation had chased him out of the church on the next Sunday morning. The living remained vacant for no more than fifteen minutes. A woman turned up on the spot and founded a UFO-church in the fatherless parish.

The one thing above all which bound Harprecht and Herkenrath together in this new existence was their common definition of their purpose in life: to get Reuben Hecht sent to a children's home at all costs because he was to blame for the degradation, not to say devastation of their *status quo ante bellum in omnibus*. No sacrifice was too great to achieve this, and they wore their fingers to the bone with writing while shackled together by dreary necessity. They had been compelled to swap the doctor's mansion and Prümers's vicarage for makeshift accommodation in one of the outer suburbs. It was a revolting shack which a lunatic had spent months of hard labour building right outside a small garden centre. The garden centre then immediately went bankrupt and the owners left the area. The unauthorised builder's original idea had been to open a cafe for long-distance motorists in his hut, but months of jerry-building had used up all his reserves of energy. Added to that, car-driving went completely out of fashion. The long-distance car-drivers all settled down and ate at home.

Harprecht and Herkenrath happened to be passing that Sunday afternoon and the lunatic was standing outside his shack with a look on his face as if he were about to gargle with bricks. The three of them started talking although, naturally, a rational conversation was impossible with the lunatic, who very much resembled Swinnskjöll *père*, but could not actually be him because the police had disposed of the latter the previous evening. In his deluded state he attacked Herkenrath, accusing him of having written some defamatory newspaper article or other. Enough, he said, was enough, going after Herkenrath like a berserk gorilla. Harprecht muttered something about having to get along and gave definite signs of being about to leave. However, one second before the furious lunatic could get his hands on his victim, who was backing away in alarm, the air was suddenly rent with a noise like the sound of a centrifugal pump. Something dark and indefinable which, one moment later, wasn't there any more, seemed to be aimed directly at the frenzied unfortunate. He was disabled and dismantled, disconnected, disarticulated, disassembled and totally destroyed. The only thing that was left of him was his shack.

At first Harprecht and Herkenrath thought of moving into the abandoned living quarters of the garden-centre buildings, but they quickly came to see that that was impossible. All the rooms had been taken over by swampy jungle. It looked very much as if the offspring of the hothouse plants left behind by the former owners had mutated. The water and electricity had been cut off, so they obviously must have found some other source of energy, though what it was remained a mystery. Certainly the tropical trees and creepers were flourishing, turning the rooms into extensive landscapes. In one corner of what had presumably been the living-room was a wooden hut with a thatched roof. All in all it looked very inviting, but in the neighbouring room Harprecht and Herkenrath found a curled-up python. And the door between the two rooms wouldn't shut any more because of some thick roots and a banana tree growing though it. Anyway, in the damp, unhealthy climate the door had become irremediably warped. There was nothing for it but to make do with the revolting shack.

'Doomed we are, doomed to die,' said the ex-theologian.

Harprecht said nothing. It was hours before they managed to pluck up the courage to go inside the lunatic's edifice, which, despite everything, was reasonably solid, even partly made of roughly plastered brick. Finally they overcame their qualms. The things that met their apprehensive gaze in the interior were, without exception, dusty and dog-eared, mildewed and slightly foxed, but otherwise in sound condition. Most of the dirt and all the coloured pencil drawings turned out to be erasable. Strangely enough, there was also electricity and running water. The lunatic had seen to everything, only his strength had run out before he got a licence for his long-distance-drivers' snack-bar. As his diaries made clear, the abolition of the motor car, and therefore of long-distance car journeys, had completely unhinged him. However, the fridge was empty, not the least scrap of food could be found.

'And no booze in the house,' Harprecht observed.

Neither of them had any money. Getting in even the most basic supplies was going to be a hazardous undertaking. On the other side of the street were the only shops in the district, a bakery and a lottery kiosk. On the Monday no one was prepared to allow them credit. They let themselves be shooed out of the bakery without putting up much resistance, but they showed more determination at the lottery kiosk. They spent an eternity hanging round the huge selection of magazines, waiting for a chance to grab at least one of the smutty publications. They couldn't get anywhere near the miniature bottles of spirits on the shelf behind the counter, the owner was keeping a close watch on them. Having achieved nothing with cunning, Harprecht and Herkenrath went over to open warfare. They kept on whining and moaning until the owner could stand it no longer. Eventually, to get rid of them, he made them an offer. He pointed to a transparent container full of lurid shiny cards coated with patches of an abradable substance among the fatuous pictures printed on them. He was willing, he said, to let them have one of these lottery tickets, valued at one mark, gratis, that is to give them a fair chance of getting rich, if they for their part would give a written undertaking never to pester him again. Harprecht demanded an additional clause in the contract to the effect that even if they won the jackpot, the kiosk owner would not sue them for a share. With his great experience of the lottery, the kiosk owner had no problem signing something like that. The tickets in the transparent plastic container were sure to be blanks; at most the two pests would win a free go or a couple of marks. Even he assumed that the stories of big wins were just marketing hype. It was as good as impossible to find any ticket worth much at all in that glittering pile of hazardous waste.

Once the two parties were in possession of their legally signed and witnessed copies, they proceeded to the draw. Harprecht shoved Herkenrath to one side and plunged his arm into the lottery tickets. He spent a long time rummaging around. The kiosk owner pointedly remarked that he closed at half past six. It was beginning to look doubtful whether Harprecht would ever take his arm out of the container. But then he did. Earnestly he handed the ticket he had selected with such conscientious care over for his partner to perform the manual labour.

Using a flat, red plastic triangle, Herkenrath scraped the coating off the card at the places indicated, revealing various sums in Deutschmarks printed underneath. If there were three of the same, then the owner of the ticket won that amount. On Harprecht and Herkenrath's ticket it was *50,000.00 DM*. The owner of the kiosk had a nervous breakdown and the lucky winners immediately set about stocking up with food, a typewriter and a colour television with a satellite dish. Although they were now gratifyingly solvent, they were still frustrated. So frustrated that they even watched wrestling every day on one of the idiot channels. Before they went to sleep they would imagine in vivid detail how they would send Reuben to a home and maltreat him.

Whenever the typewriter was occupied because Herkenrath was writing a letter to his publishers, or when the results of all the psychological tests, together with commentaries and alternative scoring systems, had been sent off to the newspapers or magazines, Harprecht would prowl round the premises of the old garden centre. Herkenrath, who, as a self-styled 'animal and nature writer', ought to have been very interested in these excursions, never accompanied him.

One day Harprecht reported, possibly as a result of an hallucination, probably to make himself seem important, that he had seen a woman. Like lightning she had climbed up a tree in the room beyond the non-closing door.

'She was wearing a leopard-skin bikini, was slim, fair-complexioned and had long, red hair. Her feet were dyed blue,' he told Herkenrath in solemn tones. Despite his aching head, he wanted to know at once who the woman might have been. As a nature writer, he said, Herkenrath must be acquainted with the denizens of the forest. Why not with those of the jungle?

'Would you mind just waiting until I've finished my letter,' was all the answer he got. The letter said:

Dear Sir,

I heard, I was told that for some time now you have gone over to specialising in medical handbooks and treatises. I believe that this can only have been an 'intermediate stage', 'the snows of yesteryear' so to speak, if I have hit the nail on the head.

In my bygone correspondence – you have so far never replied – I offered you a number of good, important manuscripts from my pen. Among them was my volume of animal fables which, it now occurs to me, almost deserves to be called a medical tome. I would have a look at it some time. I have the feeling you are not really on the right track with medical handbooks and treatises. Perhaps you should reconsider.

Time presses, so I must end there.

I remain, sir, your obedient servant,

Herkenrath

Harprecht explained his problem once more.

'That,' replied Herkenrath in schoolmasterish tones, 'will have been one of the white goddesses of the jungle. These women are wild and indomitable, they are more than a match for lions and tigers, panthers and elephants. The superstitious savages stand in fear and awe of them and submit to them with slavish deference.'

Harprecht wanted to know everything about them, and in great detail.

'In that case I'll have to consult a reference book,' said Herkenrath, groaning as he pulled a cardboard box out from underneath his camp-bed. It was the wrong one, the one containing the evaluations of the psychological tests as well as the carbons of his letters to the publishers. The next box but one turned out to be the right one. In it were his reference works in genuine Brimlingham editions of 1974. The article 'Jungle heroines' in the volume *I Spy in the Forest*, contained the following names:

Sheena, Rulah, Camilla, Cave Girl, Jann of the Jungle, Jungle Lil, Lorna, Princess Pantha, Saäri, Tiger Girl, Tygra and *Zegra.*

It was specifically emphasised that there were a number of others, but those listed were the more important ones. Moreover, according to the book they were all blondes, apart from Rulah, who had black hair. There was no mention of a red-haired jungle queen or goddess. Harprecht threw himself into the study of these names, giving himself over to reckless speculation and much counting of syllables. Several times Herkenrath told his companion to restrain himself, in the end he even had to knock him down. However, his own curiosity had been raised, so he accompanied Harprecht on his next excursion into the former living quarters of the garden centre. He was amazed at the extent to which they had spread. The jungle seemed to stretch boundlessly into depths which defied the laws of nature. And out of these boundless depths a figure was slowly coming towards them.

'Is that your jungle goddess?' asked Herkenrath.

Harprecht wasn't sure. They had to wait until they had a clearer view. No, they realised after a while, that wasn't a red-haired woman in a leopard-skin bikini. It was a man in a white shirt and grey trousers. When he had come close enough for them to see that he was about thirty years old, he called out to them,

'Hey! You there! My name is Sondergeld. Would this be the long-distance-drivers' snack bar? It can't be far from here?'

'My dear fellow,' replied Herkenrath, 'I'm afraid you're too late. The long-distance drivers have all settled down and are thus no longer an economically significant group. The snack bar was never finished.'

'But that's why I'm here,' said the man calling himself Sondergeld. 'I'm going to found the Movement for the Revival of the Long-Distance Driver. It's my destiny. I shall live in the uncompleted snack-bar building.'

Harprecht and Herkenrath immediately vetoed this idea:

'No, there's no room.'

'*We* live there.'

A menacing look appeared on Sondergeld's face. 'You can live in this thatched hut here,' he growled. 'It is my sacred duty to complete the long-distance-drivers' snack bar and to lead the Revival Movement from there. You'd better not cause any problems, I can get very nasty.'

They believed him. Thus it was that Harprecht and Herkenrath were compulsorily resettled with all their worldly goods. They were worried the tropical climate might damage the typewriter. As they lugged their cardboard boxes to the hut they told each other how lucky they were Sondergeld knew nothing about all the money they'd won. By evening they had settled into the jungle hut, in a rough and ready sort of way. There was even less room than in the revolting shack the atomised lunatic had built.

'I think I'd better write another letter to the publishers,' Herkenrath muttered.

Harprecht peered into the bushes. Perhaps he'd get another glimpse of the mysterious woman? Instead of her, it was Sondergeld he saw coming in through the living-room door. He'd brought a few bottles of blended rum, so they had to be nice to him.

'Gentlemen,' he announced, with a radiant smile, 'I have not been idle. The Movement for the Revival of the Long-Distance Driver has grown enormously; there are already sixty-two members. Unfortunately, we have to remain an underground movement, which means we cannot apply for charitable status and the tax concessions that brings.'

Proudly he showed them the list and poured them some rum. Harprecht and Herkenrath had no choice but to familiarise themselves with the goals of the movement. A three-pronged campaign was planned:

1. Long-distance driving must be revived.
2. The power of the bus-drivers must be broken.
3. All power to the long-distance driver!

'The bus-drivers have procured the abolition of individual motorised travel and, most importantly, of long-distance goods transport. Our roads and motorways are entirely taken up with bus lanes,' thundered Sondergeld. 'As well as that, they have enormous influence on the music market. All heavy-metal groups are managed by bus-drivers.'

'Bus-drivers!' exclaimed Harprecht and Herkenrath as one man. Their faces twisted with rage. Wailing and stamping their feet, they told Sondergeld what they personally had suffered at the hands of bus-drivers. Soon the jungle echoed to the cry of 'Cursèd be all bus-drivers!' in three-part harmony.

Sondergeld wondered how he could transform the hatred felt by the two victims of bus-driver violence into a love of long-distance motoring. If he could do that he would have won two more converts for the Movement. It wasn't going to be easy. True, they had nothing personal *against* long-distance drivers, but there were serious prejudices to combat. And now they had been kicked out of their dwelling to make room for the Movement as well. Showing them photos of particularly handsome long-distance drivers or trucks wouldn't do much good. All Sondergeld could do for the moment was to keep their glasses filled with rum and get them worked up about bus-drivers. When things had gone as far as they could go in that direction, Harprecht changed the subject.

'Where was it you were coming from when we met you in the jungle, Herr Sondergeld?' he asked.

A strangely transfigured, not to say foolish look appeared on their visitor's face; it wasn't an easy question for him to answer.

'That's a funny question. I can't remember having been anywhere. Haven't I always been here, where I belong, working for the Revival of the Long-Distance Driver? I'm surprised you say you met me in the jungle and I was coming from somewhere ... But look how the Movement's grown again. Eighty-one members already!'

The list had indeed got longer.

'He's two pfennigs short of a mark,' thought Harprecht and Herkenrath, quickly downing another glass of rum.

'I shall go to every bus-station,' declared Sondergeld in solemn tones. 'I shall win over some of the bus-drivers to the Movement. Tell me, is that not bold? Or heroic? Say, "We think that's heroic," and, "What a devil of a fellow, he's actually going into the lion's den!" Go on, say it. Now! Or there'll be no more rum.'

106

'We've already had enough as it is,' they muttered. 'We have that ominous feeling round our heads.'

'Well I've got some help for you, you useless pair,' squawked Sondergeld, grabbed the last, only half-dead bottle and staggered out of the hut. With a cry of 'All power to the long-distance driver!' he left the jungle. Despite the late hour he slammed the door shut behind him with a loud crash.

'If things continue like this,' said Harprecht, 'we can't go on living here.'

'Perhaps he won't be the man he is now,' said Herkenrath, 'once the bus-drivers have finished with him.'

Next morning they had sufficiently recovered to go to the bakery. Their skulls were still throbbing from the previous evening's overindulgence in blended rum. The light in the open air almost killed them and the things they then saw and heard outside the garden centre were beyond belief. Dozens of strangers, several bus-drivers in uniform among them, were sitting on the ground. All were paying reverent attention to the words of a woman standing on the cabin of a juggernaut, preaching.

'If that's Sondergeld, then he really isn't the same person,' said Harprecht.

Herkenrath recognised the woman. 'That's not Sondergeld,' he said, 'that's the UFO priestess who took over the congregation I had as Pastor Prümers.'

A sign had been attached to the revolting shack:

LONG-DISTANCE-DRIVERS' SNACK BAR AND HEAD OFFICE OF THE MOVEMENT FOR THE REVIVAL OF THE LONG-DISTANCE DRIVER

Every time they applauded the preacher the assembled gathering set up a chant:

'The long-distance driver has spoken. The power of the bus-drivers must be broken. All power to the long-distance driver!'

'What's she got to do with the Movement?' hissed Herkenrath peevishly.

'What on earth's she on about, anyway?' asked Harprecht peevishly.

The woman spake thus:

'Herr Sondergeld has certainly taken considered pains with his work. In legends, hagiographies, switching and theology he has bound himself to the task of extracting everything of long-distance driving that can bind to ufology. That goes much farther than the explanation now classics of long-distance driverers as forecursors of ufonauts.'

The crowd chanted, 'The long-distance driver has spoken. The power of the bus-drivers must be broken. All power to the long-distance driver!'

'But,' the preacher continued, 'what is very rapidly striking is the type of conception whom have been taken in by Herr Sondergeld: legendary facts alternating with ufological attestations without great interpretation. It is clearly that Herr Sondergeld has valued the apparent parallelism of the two type's of conditions as sufficing unto themselves. One cannot be angry with him at this in these days in which some interpret over their own hypotheses. The expert values his learning, the layman will be sensitive by the difference of the facts, by the symbolic wealth of small tangentials through which Herr Sondergeld leads us onto spheres which, notwithstanding, match us with thick foliage. The great fountainhead for modern myth finds its continuation in the importance accorded the symbol of the long-distance driver. It is these symbols, these hidden conceptions, sometimes malformed or carried out to reality, which convey to us knowledge of fraternal ship in long-distance driver to and with helpings of UFO phenomena.'

Again there was a chorus of 'The long-distance driver has spoken. The power of the bus-drivers must be broken. All power to the long-distance driver!'

The UFO priestess was coming to the end of her address.

'In the end, the power of the long-distance driver will be transmitted by varying colours of the UFOs of alternating presence of guardian spiriting as well as degravitation phenomena or deweighting, invulnerabilising, particularmost this propulsion by bounding. Thus, ultimately, Herr Sondergeld's praiseworthy modesty in time is the doctrine of rediscovering traces and gladly making the secret from long-distance driver to extraterrestrial: all power to the long-distance driver!'

The horn of the juggernaut was sounded with shameless abandon as the whole company roared out its three-piece creed.

'What on earth's going on at your place over there?' was the question Harprecht and Herkenrath were confronted with as soon as they entered the baker's. They feigned ignorance and, blushing, just quietly bought their rolls. When they crossed over to the other side of the road again they found that they were not allowed back into the garden-centre premises.

'It's all been taken over by the Revival Movement,' they were told.

'But we live here.'

'Nonsense. Only Herr Sondergeld lives here. And the Movement. We are the Movement!'

'But we lived here before Herr Sondergeld.'

Things that happened before Herr Sondergeld's arrival, they were informed in harsh and vitriolic tones, did not count. Herr Sondergeld's arrival was the beginning of a new era, one sod cut by him was worth a million.

'Bus-driver sympathisers, are we?' said someone clearly suffering from a compulsive and object-specific need for action. Harprecht and Herkenrath protested vigorously against any such imputation.

But all their protests were in vain and the cry of 'Bus-driver sympathisers!' rang out. They would have been struck down or strung up if a cohort of the Bus-Drivers' Rapid Reaction Unit had not arrived. In the chaos that immediately broke out Harprecht and Herkenrath managed to escape with their rolls and find refuge in the garden centre. Behind them the Rapid Reaction Unit were mercilessly laying into anyone and everyone unfortunate enough to get in their way. It looked like the end of the Revival Movement. The shack with its provocative 'Long-Distance-Drivers' Snack Bar' sign was already being razed to the ground.

Back in the thatched hut Harprecht and Herkenrath hastily gathered together all their cardboard boxes, their typewriter, television and everything else they had in the way of possessions.

'We've got to get away,' panted Harprecht. 'If the Bus-Drivers' Rapid Reaction Unit catches us here we'll be put up against the wall and shot, or at least put in a home.'

'But we had nothing at all to do with the business,' whined Herkenrath.

'That wouldn't bother them. We live right next to the Movement's offices, we drank Sondergeld's rum and we don't like bus-drivers. That's all that counts.'

They loaded up their goods and chattels, and hurried off blindly in the direction Sondergeld had come from.

III

At the Holzhindenburg bus-station Edwina discovered that her travel money had been devalued, with the result that, for financial reasons, she could not travel as an adult.

'I'll have to buy a child's ticket,' she told Reuben, 'we've got enough for that. Anyway, if I travel as a child I'll last longer. That way I kill two birds with one stone. From now on I'm your little sister, OK?'

It was only with the greatest reluctance that Reuben agreed.

'Don't look so bloody pissed off, Sondergeld,' said Edwina and went to get changed.

That was the last straw! Reuben had so looked forward to travelling with an attractive young woman, and now this. It was definitely time for a quick exit. Now, while she was in the ladies' getting changed, was his opportunity. He took the provisions with him. After just three steps he heard a familiar female voice calling, 'Well then, young man, where are we off to?'

Reuben thought Edwina had caught him in the act. Shamefacedly he turned round, already preparing a flimsy excuse. Behind him, however, he saw not Edwina but the pallid blondes' white minibus. It was the driver's voice he had heard, of course.

'Oh,' said Reuben, 'anywhere as long as it's away from here.'

In his desperation he hoped they would take him

with them, but it would have to be quick because Edwina might be back at any moment. The driver showed no signs of wanting to offer him a lift, but this was an emergency. He would have to ask her himself. Before he got round to it, however, the pallid beauty asked him, 'Have you still got our magic token?'

Yes, he still had it. He automatically patted his jacket[1] over the tin in the inside pocket. He had forgotten all about the mysterious hair. Then, just like the last time they met, the driver said, 'Great! Keep it up! But if you'll excuse us now, we have to get on.'

'Stop!' shouted Reuben. 'Take me with you!'

But the window had already been wound up and the minibus was disappearing into the distance. It was almost a case of déjà vu. What could be behind these obviously pointless meetings with the four women who claimed to be the Flesh-eating Fetish Bitches? As he said the last time, *he was starting to get sick and tired of all this mystification! What was it about him that made everyone treat him like that?* Did he still have time to slip away? No, dammit! The door to the ladies' opened and Edwina returned. Once more she was the pretty, slightly oriental-looking six-year-old.

'You still look bloody pissed off,' she said to Reuben. 'Now we've got to go and buy the tickets. You'll have to do that, you're the older one.'

There were difficulties. Tickets to the Colony were

---

[1] Gronius and Rauschenbach would have formulated it thus: 'He thwacked his leather jerkin.'

not sold to minors. Children and young persons were allowed to travel unaccompanied by a grown-up, but tickets had to be purchased and collected by adults.

'So we can say goodbye to the trip,' said Reuben.

'Not at all,' replied Edwina. She'd just have to change twice, then that hurdle would be behind them as well. A blasted nuisance, but not impossible. Thus, contrary to expectation, Reuben had a further chance of escaping. Two, to be exact.

Before Edwina could reach the door to the ladies', the bus-station suddenly keeled over and was up the spout. It couldn't have been the work of the Long-Distance Drivers' Revival Movement, since that was not to be founded until a few days later. Oh, bugger chronology! It was definitely an attack by the militant wing of the Revival Movement. As if by a miracle, neither Reuben nor Edwina, nor anyone else was injured. They even managed to lever one of the buses back onto its wheels. The three drivers asked the boy and the little girl if they would like to go with them to the next bus-station, which was called 'Kroatenundblitzen'. Edwina naturally accepted the kind offer. Reuben was so cheesed off that, like Herr Mozart before him, he wished he would get an attack of nettlerash-fever. His last hope was that when they reached Kroatenundblitzen his companion would have to go and change before buying the tickets. If he couldn't escape then, he deserved everything he got. He climbed on the bus.

A sunset glow was switched on, filling the bus with reds and golds. With her luggage Edwina scrambled into the seat behind the drivers. A dreadfully disappointed Reuben sat next to her, the sack of provisions on his knees, and didn't say a word during the whole journey. He was concocting plans of revenge while Edwina was trying to guess which of the steering units was in operation. Before they arrived at Kroatenundblitzen she ticked number 2 on the list. Reuben, who always chose number 2, made no exception this time, despite his bad mood. And which red light should go on at the end of the journey but the one on dashboard number 2! No one apart from them had chosen it, so Edwina and Reuben each won a child's ticket to the Colony. An incredible coincidence, wouldn't you say?!

In contrast to Edwina, Reuben was not pleased at all. For the third time his pissed-offness was a matter for comment. How else was he expected to look? Now his only hope was that the requirements of her bodily functions would force the girl to go to the ladies'. Or should *he* pretend to need to go and quietly exit through a rear door or a window?

First of all they got off. Immediately opposite was a very large InterCountry coach, ready to leave. The sign declaring it to be the only direct, non-stop connection from Kroatenundblitzen to the Colony that day was unmissable. The three bus-drivers shouted to the young prizewinners to hurry up if they wanted to get on, now that they had those splendid free tickets. Edwina ran on ahead. Reuben had to follow with the provisions willy-nilly. Given the circumstances it was impossible for him to make a dash for it, his last chance had gone. If only there had been a crush of passengers between the two buses in which he could have submerged without trace, but no, he was the sole figure there and was already expected on the other side. And not just by Edwina, who was already on the steps of the gigantic vehicle; the six drivers and several conductors and conductresses were giving the laggard impatient looks.

Many new features had been introduced into the construction of InterCountry coaches which had originally been developed for spacecraft and space-stations. Thanks to the unlimited power of the bus-drivers, constructors and visionaries from the field of space travel had been transferred to coach production. The result was buses that were almost as big as passenger ships and looked like intergalactic transports from the covers of science-fiction magazines.

'Are you two travelling all on your own?' asked one of the conductresses as she punched their free tickets.

'Yes,' replied Reuben, 'our big sister's going to meet us at the frontier.'

He said that in order to try and force Edwina to change after they had arrived. It was, of course, pure wishful thinking. The conductress completely ignored his superfluous comment. There were no restrictions whatever placed on travellers who had won tickets as prizes, no certification from parents or legal guardians was necessary, there was no requirement to be accompanied by an adult. Another woman, a kind of stewardess, even led the young passengers to two very nice reclining seats on the first floor. Edwina was delighted. Reuben had to grin and bear it to avoid further censure for his woebegone expression.

'In ten hours we'll be there. And we've saved the money for the journey,' said Edwina with satisfaction. 'When we get to the Colony,' she went on, 'we can buy the things you need. I just don't understand how someone can set off without any luggage at all. It's not a day trip, you know.'

Reuben just said, 'Yes, yes.' His minder put her seat back, made herself comfortable and went to sleep. That way she saved more energy so she would last even longer. Reuben treated himself to a glass of rum and half a block of marzipan from the provisions. Immediately everything looked better. He realised it was a good thing he was travelling to the Colony. He really could begin a new life over there, a completely new life. He'd manage to shake off Edwina somehow or other. It was really quite funny that he should end up in the place his father had always intended him to go, even if under rather different circumstances. As if it were all 'predetermined'. Fortunately his current situation differed from his father's plans in one crucial point. He was not going to the Colony as an official illustrator. Oh no, not at all. That gave him a sense of great satisfaction. He was an adventurer going out into the world to seek his fortune. Once he had given her the slip, Edwina could hunt for Scherer-Dextry's lactically generated androids by herself. She was asleep. That was good, it meant at least he didn't have to make conversation with her. If she had made the journey as the woman she had on occasion been, he would definitely have made her the object of his attentions, but as things were . . .

Thanks to the invigorating effect of the rum, he felt strong enough to cope with the television programmes on offer. The only channel available on board InterCountry coaches was the bus-drivers' channel, and that was just as lousy as all the rest.

As he watched, Reuben kept recognising people he'd known twenty years ago, when they'd been the same age as him. Now in their late thirties, they occupied important positions, some in the ranks of of the reporters, others among the reportees. At the beginning of the year a former schoolfriend of his called Schlüter had been in the news. Late on the morning of the second (!) of January he had gone round to his neighbour's house and shot him through the closed front door. Despite repeated requests since the New Year, the latter had refused to stop celebrating and had continued to bawl out songs and let off fireworks. Schlüter had been acquitted.

There was also a girl from his class whom Reuben had already seen on television. She had changed her name to Furlene and was a general nuisance with her silly dancing and singing.

When Reuben switched on the bus TV they were showing the Sunday edition of a regional magazine programme. The presenter was also someone he had known twenty years ago. In those days she could eat the glass from spectacles, now she was working for the local television channel. After a report about a man who, by his own admission, could imagine *anything*, came the regional news: murder, manslaughter,

121

child abuse, arson, terrorism and floods. Then a picture of Reuben's father suddenly filled the screen, accompanied by the following report:

We have just received a report that the distinguished anthropologist Lehmann Hecht and his wife have been found dead at their home.

(Wedding photo of the Hechts.)

The cause of death has in both cases been clearly established as suicide. There is no obvious reason, nor did the couple leave a suicide note. The police are assuming it was a spontaneous action, possibly triggered off by domestic problems.

(Shot of the house.)

In the course of their investigations the police discovered that all the taps in the house had been unscrewed, air pumped into the pipes and the taps then screwed back on again.

(Shots taken inside the house followed by a photo of Lehmann Hecht.)

Neighbours stated that during the last few weeks the specialist in primate research had become completely fused with his bed. Problems of a professional nature have not been ruled out. Many years ago Lehmann Hecht is said to have gone to the Colony as a hopeless case to study the aboriginals there.

The Hechts leave a son, Reuben, a minor who has vanished without trace.

There followed a photo of Reuben with a description. Any passenger who saw the programme was bound to recognise him. This fact hit him harder than the death of his parents. He'd never liked them anyway. So, apart from the rubbish about his supposed guilt, Rossman and Prümers had been telling the truth. At least that point had been cleared up. It only made his current situation even more desperate. Not only did he have Harprecht, Herkenrath and the police on his trail, now viewers throughout the country could join in the hunt for him. He had to get to the Colony without being recognised at all costs. But how? Plastic surgery was a non-runner from the start and he didn't have a mask with him, not even a pair of sunglasses or a false beard. And anyway, how could he have explained such a disguise to Edwina? Thank God she hadn't seen the news. The next transmission was a programme of sausage poetry for bus-drivers.

'That's odd,' said a man's voice behind Reuben, 'this screen's still working.'

In a trice Reuben had hidden his face in his hands. Peeking through his fingers, he turned round and saw an unknown man, another passenger, standing in the aisle beckoning the stewardess over. He pointed indignantly at Reuben's screen.

'How is it that this television's working when all the others on board are kaput, hm? Answer me that, then?'

'A miracle, perhaps?' the stewardess retorted. 'Just a second, I'll soon see to it.'

She opened up the television set, more or less kneeling in Reuben's lap, fiddled around inside for a moment and immediately the screen went blank.

'There you are,' she said, 'that's that sorted. As we announced over the loudspeaker, all the sets on board are out of order today.'

Closing up the back of the television, she said to Reuben, 'Of course, you only joined the bus in Kroatenundblitzen, didn't you? That was *after* the announcement, so you can't have known. That will have been transmitted to your machine. That's why it worked.'

Satisfied with this explanation, the passenger stomped off down the aisle.

Still keeping his hands in front of his face, Reuben asked, 'So no one on board can have seen the programme that was on just now?'

'Of course not,' replied the stewardess. 'What was it?'

'Oh, the usual.' Reuben lowered his hands. 'I've already forgotten it.'

The next moment the stewardess was called away because someone wanted to recount a dream to her. Edwina was still sleeping. She probably wouldn't wake up before they arrived in the Colony.

'You can't just sit there all the time thinking about what happened to your parents,' Reuben told himself. Now he no longer needed to worry that all the passengers would recognise him, he could concentrate on enjoying the adventure. He left his seat to look round the bus. No one took any notice of him. The first thing to strike him were the signs with anti-long-distance-driver slogans. They were everywhere, like advertising in other places, or political propaganda. They mocked the now extinct species in the nastiest possible way. Apart from slogans, there were most unsavoury jokes about long-distance drivers. Reuben was not amused. Did the bus-drivers really have to trample all over their defeated opponents in this way? At one time there had been a commission of inquiry into that kind of thing and the bus-drivers had been reprimanded by the Committee on Signs in Public Life. Even among the politicians there were those who thought the bus-drivers had grown too powerful.

There was always quite a bit put on to entertain the passengers on board the InterCountry coaches. It wasn't like on the cross-Channel ferries where the passengers, after paying outrageous sums, are left with nothing to do but sit out the journey in a cata-tonic stupor or, depending on the line, go down with the boat. Reuben read the posters announcing the wealth of entertainment. There were beauty contests, master-classes in pest control, a visit to a schnapps factory, Turkish baths, horse races, a brothel, a school, a church, a posting-house, several bars, an art gallery and a concert hall. At the moment the art gallery had a Buckauer retro-spective, a fact which he studiously ignored. What he did find interesting, though, was the programme of concerts. As well as several heavy metal bands, all of which were managed by bus-drivers, the Flesh-eating Fetish Bitches were due to appear that day. Reuben had not expected to see them again so soon. He had just enough time to go to the lavatory before the scheduled start of the concert.

It appeared that the Flesh-eating Fetish Bitches

had the same idea, for the white minibus of the four mysterious blondes was standing in the wide corridor outside the ladies'. As if they could read his mind, the door opened and the four emerged. They weren't going to pull the wool over his eyes this time! He was going to grill them, and it was going to be a you're-not-getting-away-till-you've-let me-in-on-your-secret grilling. Of course this plan, based on an overestimation of his own abilities, was never carried out. Within two seconds they had him eating out of their hands. One of them showed him a record sleeve hot off the press.

'Our new LP. It's called the *100,000-Electric-Rays-from-Heaven Album of the Wonders of the World*,' she said condescendingly.

'Well I'll be an android's uncle!' Reuben exclaimed in surprise. There was no doubt at all, the sleeve had been designed by Buckauer. Having seen the one picture at Scherer-Dextry's he was well able to identify Buckauer's style anywhere, anytime.

'What a coincidence,' he said. 'I'm supposed to be doing research on Buckauer, you see.' It seemed a good strategy to spotlight that and keep quiet about his main mission.

'Research on Buckauer? Then you just have to see the retrospective in the gallery,' she advised him.

'Later perhaps. The first thing on my agenda is your concert. It's great that you're playing here today!'

'We're going to present all the material from our new album,' the quadruplets promised as they

126

climbed into their minibus. 'And now, if you'll excuse us . . .'

And with that, they were gone. Reuben's bosom was a battleground of conflicting emotions, which might have incited others to compose Tchaikovsky-style symphonies. The state of his psyche would have been a real gift to a writer as well, but he wasn't one. Nor is the author of this work, so do not expect the plumbing of emotional depths.

Reuben hurriedly relieved himself and ran down to the concert hall on the lower deck. The Flesh-eating Fetish Bitches were just starting. He paid no attention to the way they looked, nor to what they were playing. Once more he jigged about in the aisles like a puppet on a string and screamed himself hoarse. Nine hours later Edwina was shaking him and shouting, 'It's time to stop, Sondergeld. We're there.'

Reuben came to. All the lights in the concert hall were on, the audience had left, the stage was empty.

'Come on, come on, you bugger, we've got to get off the bus.' Edwina was not pleased. When the bus reached the terminus they had woken her with the news that she would have to go and collect her big brother from the concert hall. Reuben had difficulty regaining full consciousness. The last thing he could remember was his conversation with the four women.

'Buckauer . . . ,' he muttered, 'Buckauer record sleeve, Buckauer exhibition . . .'

'Is that your way of getting on with your Buckauer research when there's a window in your android programme?' asked Edwina. 'If Scherer-Dextry knew . . .' She pushed him in the direction of the exit. Her luggage and their provisions were waiting there for them.

Reuben scowled as he realised he was no nearer solving the mystery of the Flesh-eating Fetish Bitches. He had no memory of the concert whatsoever. It was always the same, as soon as the music started he was deaf to everything else. This time he'd even been deaf to the music. 'I wouldn't make a good concert reviewer,' he admitted to himself, 'but at least the journey passed quickly.'

Outside, in the cool night air, his consciousness very quickly returned, and soon he was asking himself how on earth he could have spent nine hours in that over-excited state. Other groups must have played. Could he have jigged about and screamed non-stop for the whole nine hours? It would seem so. He was retrospectively ashamed of himself. He felt wretched.

Reuben had a look around. Edwina and he were the only ones to have got out. Apart from them, no one wanted to go to the Colony. The bus set off back as quickly as possible. He saw the frontier control, a small Customs and Excise office to the left of the barrier and the clutter of signs with prohibitions and commands. It wasn't that easy to be granted entry to the Colony. The border was closely guarded by the troops of the semi-generals, Olga and Oscar Voll, as well as a detachment of the Lüneburg Heath Home Guard equipped with baking trays. A couple of minors couldn't simply stroll in and hunt for some androids generated from UHT milk for a freak show.

Reuben racked his brains feverishly as to what to do next. Item 1 on his agenda was to shake off his companion. And then what? Alas, it seemed a matter of pure chance.

'What now? I'm freezing.' That was Edwina. Reuben was forced to improvise and automatically reverted to his previous strategy. Edwina should go and change, she couldn't accompany him to the Colony as a child. She had no objection to this proposal, nor to his announced intention of going to the Customs building by himself 'to deal with the formalities for both of us.' Assuming he had sufficient accreditation and had been provided with full authorisation by Scherer-Dextry, she went off to the toilet of the frontier bus-station. That left Reuben with precisely as much time to get across to the other side as she needed to change, i.e not much at all, especially as he had no idea how to go about it. Whatever strategy he decided upon, he would have to present himself at the Customs post first. 'What on earth am I going to tell them?' he wondered nervously. He felt that the world was an untidy workshop where he was stuck in a vice which was being vigorously tightened.

'I'm just not going to manage it, they'll be onto me right away, that's for sure. Oh, what a pitiful existence.' With the thought, 'Best to be dead,'[2] he opened the wooden door to the shed.

The moment he entered he was plunged into bluish light and hot, smoky, stuffy air. On the wall opposite

[2] From 'Schwerin', Huflattich, Stümper & ff Editions no. 22.

was a television set, and it was switched on. Two border guards with congenital cigarettes dangling from the corners of their mouths were shouting down their telephones. One immediately left his desk and went into the neighbouring room. The other indicated to Reuben that he would have to wait a minute. Just when he didn't have a single second to spare! Reuben was so impatient he started kicking the desks, filing cabinets and walls. While this was going on the guard who had left was reporting to his superior officer in the next room. By this time every TV channel imaginable had carried a report on the death of the Hechts, a report in which a photo of Reuben together with a description formed an obligatory part. Reuben had been recognised.

As the border guard entered, Major Höfmeyer, the superior officer in the next room, hid a letter he had just written. It was addressed to the publishers with whom Mothorheym, the director of the Distance Learning Academy, was hoping to publish his uncouth handbook of medicine. The letter ran:

Dear Publisher,

Please do not throw this letter away before you still have not read it. I would most respectfully like to enquire whether I may send a manuscript (poems) for your esteemed consideration. Your opinion is very important to me. And point me on my future path. I would be delighted if my letter should be of interest to you. And my letter not remain unanswered any more. Criticism, a verdict from you, is unavoidable. But perhaps your verdict

will not be that unfavourable, perhaps C or even
A+. Only then will my happiness be assured.
    I remain, sir,
    your obedient servant
        Major Höfmeyer
        Border Security Service

P.S. I do not look like a poet.

Major Höfmeyer still had to write the poems.
Somehow or other they had to deal with gherkins,
noodles, the self and love, and they definitely had to
make the reader cry.

He gave the silent, saluting guard a preoccupied
look. 'Tell me now,' he said, 'do you think that
ultimately there is no escape from the self?'

His subordinate found it impossible to comment
on that, but he could announce the arrival of Hecht
junior.

'Bring him in at once,' ordered the major.

Reuben received such a warm welcome he didn't
know whether he was coming or going. Höfmeyer
began talking right away.

'I think I may say that I was a friend of your
father. Permit me to assure you of my sincerest
condolences etc etc. Naturally his death brought the
odd tear to my eye. Look at it this way: fortunate
the man who can, perhaps, find his way back to his
origins and then, at the end, laboriously enough and
full of remorse . . . and so on, and so on. What I
mean to say is this: I know about your father's plans
for you, how he wanted you to follow the career of an

131

official illustrator in the Colony. And now you have come to take up the position he intended for you. That shows proper respect, I find it touching. I will do everything in my power to accelerate the process of immigration for you. I am sure you have all the necessary qualifications, so I will not ask you to produce documentation. However – and please excuse me for bringing this up – as I know from your late father, it is unfortunately the case that for medical reasons you can never come of age. Thus I am compelled to insist, despite the sympathy I feel for you, that you be accompanied by an adult. Is there such a person? Or would you like me to arrange for one to be officially assigned to you?'

Once again there was to be no escape. Glumly Reuben replied that he was indeed accompanied by an appropriate person. As if on cue, the border guards reported a lady had arrived asking for the young man.

'Get her to sign the form for accompanying adults,' commanded Höfmeyer.

As one might imagine, Edwina made a big impression on the two guards. They gave her a comfortable chair to sit in and plied her with biscuits and liqueurs. One of them massaged her feet, the other her shoulders. Both had the highest praise for her oriental beauty. While all this was going on, Höfmeyer's question, whether she was the official companion of the young man who had come into the building earlier, was put to her. She answered in the affirmative and signed the corresponding form. While doing so, she noticed that the person she was supposed to be accompanying was not named as Sondergeld, but as Reuben Hecht. She assumed that had been arranged by the manager of the freak show as part of the commission, so she said nothing.

'This young man is fortunate indeed,' thought the border guards enviously.

Major Höfmeyer wrote down an address, which he gave to Reuben. 'Report there. You will be given preferential treatment and assigned to a researcher as illustrator.'

Reuben felt his hair stand on end, but he kept his composure.

'It was your father's wish,' Höfmeyer went on, 'to research the nature and evolution of the aboriginals together with his son. Now is the moment for you to come into your inheritance, whatever that might mean.'

As they said goodbye, he asked Reuben, 'Tell me, do you think that ultimately there is an escape from the self or not?'

Reuben would have gladly answered that he would be satisfied with escaping from his companion plus Harprecht and Herkenrath. Instead, he replied, 'I think the hassle never stops.'

Nodding reflectively, the major accompanied him to the anteroom. When he saw Edwina, he could not repress a 'Hm, not bad, not bad at all.' Reuben, the simpleton, felt this much enhanced his status. Seeing this beautiful woman again reconciled him to his situation. He was envied! Major Höfmeyer saluted.

Anyone who wanted to enter the Colony was obliged to be wormed and to undergo instant prophylactic treatment against skin parasites. With respectful bows the border guards showed Edwina and Reuben the way to the quarantine station. Meanwhile Major Höfmeyer rang the Customs and Excise doctor to announce the arrival of two prospective immigrants who were to be dealt with without delay.

The two of them were taken to individual cubicles by the sullen and half-drunk doctor. First she carried out the treatment for skin parasites. Three drops of some liquid with a revolting stench had to be massaged into their skin between their shoulder-blades, that being the one place they couldn't reach with their own tongues. Against all expectation Reuben did manage to reach it. He felt extremely queasy and threw up all over the linoleum. When, one hour later, he felt better and asked for something to eat, he was given marzipan into which the doctor had secretly worked the worming powder. This part of the treatment passed without incident. A consultation with the Customs and Excise psychologist was arranged for the following morning. Edwina and Reuben spent the night in their cubicles.

IV

Harprecht and Herkenrath were the first people to cross the jungle in a motorised vehicle, an improved, steam-driven, two-seater velocipede. In an *imaginary* vehicle, however; actually they went on foot. It was the jungle that saw the beginning of their 'self-propelling-machines phase', during which they were constantly rambling on about safety draisines, velocipede-sledges, steam velocipedes or aërocyclyes with electric engines. As they walked, they pretended to pedal and operated make-believe hand-cranks or foot-levers. In this way they got on quickly, even though they had quite a lot of luggage. Particularly important items were:

the copies of Herkenrath's letters to the publisher
the copies of Harprecht's evaluations of the
psychological tests
their reference books
the typewriter
the schnapps
the television set and, last but not least,
what was left of their winnings.

Now and then, and always just at a moment when Herkenrath simply had to look in another direction, Harprecht caught brief glimpses of the red-haired woman in the leopard-skin bikini. He was convinced she was prowling round their camp at night while he and Herkenrath were sitting, frustrated, by their fire, watching TV wrestling matches. He had a strong suspicion that it was she who had laid the extension lead, to which they connected the television, so visibly in the grass. Herkenrath, who claimed to be au fait with woodland things, was not in the least surprised to find a power supply in the jungle. But a live electrical extension lead, with no visible end in sight and current which came from an unknown source, was not a normal woodland thing.[1] When the velocipedestrians continued on their journey during the day, the extension socket retreated in front of them at the same rate at which they were proceeding. It looked as if someone was pulling it in, using it as a movable direction indicator or a lure. Like hunter-gatherers following migrating animals, Harprecht and Herkenrath followed the receding extension socket.

After they had continued in this way for several days, from one moment to the next their spectacles became totally ineffective. Instinctively Herkenrath took a few steps backwards and behold, the lenses once again corrected his short-sightedness. 'From all that we know,' he said, 'this phenomenon can only mean we've reached the border of the Colony.'

Harprecht disagreed. 'Impossible! The frontier is closely guarded by the troops of the semi-generals, Olga and Oscar Voll, as well as a detachment of the

---

[1] Nothing of the kind is mentioned in the 1974 Brimlingham edition of *I Spy in the Forest*.

Lüneburg Heath Home Guard equipped with baking trays. One can't simply stroll across it.'

And yet that must have been the case. The fact that their optical aids once more became completely useless when they went a few steps further proved it. All that Harprecht and Herkenrath could see of the country were vague, hazy shapes. The extension cable was no longer indicating their route. Trusting to luck, the pair slowly and cautiously steered their imaginary steam-velocipede through the unknown land. The appearance of an acoustic problem presented a further hindrance to their spatial orientation: only with the greatest difficulty was verbal communication possible.

'It's the time of year,' explained Herkenrath from his universal fund of knowledge. Naturally, the Colony had a different calendar. That of the aboriginals was unknown, they had never shown it to the invaders, but in the course of time it had been discovered that the year there had eight months: three months of cold, three months of heat and two months of noise. The new rulers had named the first of the noise months 'Philanthropist', in order to encourage a positive attitude on the part of the Colonists. The second noise-month was called 'Parasumi'.

So Harprecht and Herkenrath introduced conversation-memos. They are reproduced below in complete chronological order:

No. 1 (Harprecht to Herkenrath)
We must find a power supply by evening. Otherwise

how are we going to watch the TV wrestling matches?

No. 2 (Herkenrath to Harprecht)
We urgently need shelter! It's high time I wrote a letter to the publishers. Bloody having to flee like this has put a stop to everything.

No. 3 (Harprecht to Herkenrath)
With poor vision and all this noise we've as good as no chance at all. We'll probably perish miserably. It's all Reuben Hecht's fault.

No. 4 (Herkenrath to Harprecht)
Cursèd be Reuben Hecht!

No. 5 (Harprecht to Herkenrath)
And that blasted Sondergeld!

No. 6 (Herkenrath to Harprecht)
What will become of us here in the Colony if we happen *not* to perish miserably?

No. 7 (Harprecht to Herkenrath)
Since we're going through our self-propelling-machines phase, we could set up a velocipede-riding school in a suitable building.

No. 8 (Herkenrath to Harprecht)
Yes, of course! An amphicyclotheatron, a gymna-cyclidium, a velocipedrome or even a bicyclo-curriculum, why not? But where will we find a suitable building?

No. 9 (Harprecht to Herkenrath)
Large, building-like structure approx. ten yards ahead! We're heading straight for it.

No. 10 (Herkenrath to Harprecht)
Emergency stop! It *is* a building. I can feel it. The plate underneath the bell says 'Asthma & Pastrami'.[2]

No. 11 (Harprecht to Herkenrath)
That's what you think! It says 'Worldchild & Kneerider'. I'll ring the bell.

No. 12 (Herkenrath to Harprecht)
No response. The door isn't locked, let's go in. If it's quieter inside we'll occupy the building.

No. 13 (Harprecht to Herkenrath)
Should we not at least take the trouble to park our velocipede properly?

No. 14 (Herkenrath to Harprecht)
No. I hereby declare our self-propelling-machines phase concluded.

Inside the building it was pleasantly quiet, so no further conversation-memos were written. Harprecht scrutinised the furnishings. 'Typical Colonial style,' he said.

'We stay here,' declared Herkenrath and looked

---

[2] Gangsters in a film with Barbara Stanwyk and Gary Cooper.

for a comfortable spot where he could continue his work as a nature writer. The cardboard boxes, typewriter and rum were placed within easy reach. Harprecht assumed responsibility for plugging in the television set. None of the usual channels could be received in the Colony. There was only one transmitter, and that was run by the occupying power. Since it operated as a public-service broadcasting station, it was unlikely to have daily wrestling matches. After they had recovered from the shock, Harprecht and Herkenrath had to admit that without spectacles that worked they could hardly watch television anyway. At least Herkenrath could just about make out the letters on the typewriter and the things he wrote. Harprecht found reading and evaluating the small print of the psychological tests even more difficult. But there was no point in complaining, it had to be done, however red and sore it made his eyes. After all, they had to earn their living. At least that was what he told himself.

There was news on the television. When they heard the names Worldchild and Kneerider, Harprecht and Herkenrath went as close to the screen as they could. Screwing up their eyes, they saw two male portraits done in the naturalistic manner. More interesting was the sound that went with them:

'For years Worldchild and Kneerider have been carrying on their nefarious activities in the Colony disguised as a travelling brass band. Whenever their ID was checked by the aboriginals, they used old pawn tickets as well as photocopies of pawn tickets and a semi-direct certificate from the Compensation Office as documentation. For special situations they had a supply of cocktail dresses ready, knowing the aboriginals would give their eye-teeth for them. That is all over now. As far as can be reconstructed, their last day went as follows: Worldchild and Kneerider were sitting in their house, smearing aluminium acetate over each other's faces. At 11 a.m. the aboriginals arrived with angry complaints about the automatic chief Worldchild and Kneerider had sold them the previous day. Since then they have disappeared without trace.'

A half-full jar of aluminium acetate was still standing on the kitchen table, on the floor in the hall was a cocktail dress. Somewhere there was a note with something about androids generated from milk.

'I shouldn't think they're coming back,' said Harprecht. 'The building belongs to us now.'

Herkenrath was already writing another letter to the publishers:

To the publisher
Dear Sir
In my last letter I once more drew your attention to some of my manuscripts, in particular to my book of animal/medical fables. As far as quality is concerned, the only comparison in this sector of literature is Goethe or, as the case may be, Christina

Rosetti. A quite exclusive work, nothing similar has so far appeared on the market.

In fact I was extremely astonished not to receive an answer on your part, since on my part the correspondence was conducted in a passable, indeed I think I may say pleasant manner. Now I hear from a third party that medical handbooks and treatises have become the main focus of your activities.

I would therefore like to offer-for-publication two new medically relevant projects, which could also be entitulated medical publications. It all depends on the position of the observer.

1.) EIGHT HUNDRED NEW HUNTING BALLADS (BALLADS OF NATURE MAGIC)

In spite of my domination of the hunting-ballad genre in the German-speaking world (which I covered more than in extenso in most of my letters) I do not wish at this point to go into further detail.

Since you evidently make heavy weather of nature poetry and have turned, as one might suspect, to experimental works (medical handbooks and treatises) I would like to offer you today, apart from the aforementioned volume of MODERN animal/medical fables, my slim volume of poems!

2.) WHY FOX AND DACHSHUND CANNOT BEAR ANY DREADS AT ALL

The title is addressed first and foremost to the younger generation with their problems, their anxieties and anything else that might touch on those things. What we have here is what one might call 'more practical' , or let us say MORE APPLIED *poetry! There are some comforting things in it, and medical matters play a self-evident role.*

I would describe this book of poems as a small volume with a big future, containing as it does factors which at all periods have revolved around very similar fundamental problems. Consequently I would call it a guide, a manual, a primer for living. The medical component is unmistakable. In my expert opinion, every line would do honour to any advanced school reader.

So much for the moment to another side of my authorship than my balladesque self-evidences and dominations, which you will certainly and probably have extremely bored.

On that telling note I will close.

Yes, I would very much like to send you this 'duo' for your consideration.

Is it correct that your publishing house, as I have recently been told, comes from Leipzig?

Thanking you in anticipation of your esteemed reply,

> *I remain, sir,*
> *your obedient servant,*
> > *Herkenrath (editor)*

As luck would have it, there was a letter-box diagonally opposite (outside the building, unfortunately). In the section of the Colony where Harprecht and Herkenrath had ended up there happened to be a functioning postal service. Herkenrath grasped the addressed but unstamped envelope between his teeth, ran out of the house, holding his hands over his ears, and posted it. He had to lift up the flap with his nose and insert the letter without manual assistance. Harprecht stood at the living-room window observing the lengthy process. Eventually Herkenrath returned, with abrasions to his nose, chafed lips and bright-red ears.

V

The next morning the Customs and Excise doctor woke Edwina and Reuben before she started work. After various documents had been issued, they were sent down to the cellar, without any breakfast, for their consultation with the Customs and Excise psychologist. The latter was a delightful old gentleman with thick but ineffective spectacles, trembling hands and a collection of cardboard boxes. He asked Edwina and Reuben to tear up a few magazines. Analyses of their spinal fluid and countless EEGs he merely indicated with gestures and his hat. Then he sent the two of them away. Their independent existence had not been extinguished in the cellar. They had to pay 97.00 DM at the cash-desk and the barrier was raised. On the other side Edwina hired a car, which pleased Reuben, since at least it meant she couldn't go round as a little girl. To drive a car you had to be at least eighteen years old, that was the law in the Colony. She wasn't too happy with this, since she would use up a lot of energy; she would only be able to save a little at nights.

'It's awfully noisy all of a sudden,' complained Reuben. The air was kicking up a racket. Edwina explained that it was Parasumi at the moment, the second noise month. According to the calendar that had been handed out with their immigration papers, the first noise month, Philanthropist by name, had just ended. So there was a whole month of din to

come. Well informed as she was, Edwina knew that it
was quiet inside buildings. Reuben thought it over.
Should they stay in an hotel until the end of the
month? If they did, though, Edwina would go back
to being a six-year-old girl. The solution to the problem, or so it seemed to him, lay in a lengthy visit to
Worldchild and Kneerider, the discoverers of the lactically generated androids. They could move in there
for a month, and because there would be witnesses,
Edwina would have to retain her adult persona. Now
that she was back in that form, Reuben had abandoned the idea of running away. Going to see Worldchild and Kneerider first of all seemed the obvious
course of action to Edwina. Who else? It was they
who had tipped Scherer-Dextry off, so they would
surely have further information.

'Do you have their address?' asked Reuben.

Edwina had, and off they drove. Reuben took a
large mouthful of rum. He sang, 'This is the life, this
life so free, with brolly, bowler and hope,' Worms and
skin parasites kept well away from the pair. Edwina
drove without the aid of maps or town plans. She
took her bearings from the old trousers of failed
cartographers which were now lying in the sand,
exposed to wind and weather, and which represented
geographical facts. Acoustic conditions inside the car
were bearable if they kept the doors and windows
closed. There was neither hide nor hair of the aboriginals to be seen anywhere. What did suddenly
appear on the carriageway was a patrol. The road
was blocked off with baking trays.

'Obviously a detachment of the Lüneburg Heath

Home Guard,' Edwina remarked. She brought the hired car to a halt.

'Who goes there?' 'Where from?' and 'Where to?' were the questions that were asked, and papers had to be produced. They were heading for Worldchild and Kneerider, were they? That wasn't possible, there had been an incident, Worldchild and Kneerider had gone missing. Probably for good. Something to do with the aboriginals. Who since then had been restless, so that visitors were not permitted to travel round the Colony under their own steam. State of emergency.

Because of the noise they all had to shout quite loudly. So they used conversation-memos. It was made clear to Edwina and Reuben that if they couldn't provide an alternative address, for their own safety they would be taken back to the border and deported. Reuben wasn't at all happy with that idea. On the other side the police and worse were waiting for him. So for want of anything else he was forced to rummage through his pockets and pull out the piece of paper on which Major Höfmeyer had written the address of the State Research Institute where the student of official illustration was to report. No objection was raised to that. Edwina and Reuben were escorted there by the Home Guard unit with fixed baking trays. There was nothing to report on the way there.

At the Bureau for the Allocation of Official Illustrators, which had its headquarters in Neu-Worpswede, the capital of the Colony, they had to give their details to an unfriendly porter and then wait for hours in an ugly vestibule. Finally Reuben's name was called.

'Keep an eye on the provisions,' he told Edwina before disappearing into the office, where his papers were checked by a sharp-edged lady official in uniform. It was awkward that he had no certificates at all to show for his training.

'You claim to have been studying at the Holy German Paintbrush Distance Learning Academy for twenty years? I think I will just check whether that is correct,' the official snarled.

She dialled the Brunswick number of the Distance Learning Academy and a voice from the registry answered. Yes, she was willing to confirm over the telephone that Reuben Hecht's statement corresponded to the facts. To make it official, they arranged for written confirmation to be prepared.

The uniformed lady continued to interrogate Reuben. 'Have you any references? Is there anyone who can vouch for you? If not, you will be detained on remand until the written confirmation arrives.'

Major Höfmeyer was the name that occurred to him and clearly impressed the official. Breathing heavily, she grabbed the telephone and called the border post. She asked for Höfmeyer. When he replied, she put her question to him in a most obsequious manner. For a while she listened in silence, concentrating entirely on what was being said at the other end of the line. Then she scowled, slammed down the receiver and leant back. To Reuben she said not a word.

'What did he say?' he asked cautiously.

Instead of answering, she gathered up all the documents and swept into the neighbouring room, where she stayed a considerable time. Reuben wondered what Edwina would think of being kept waiting outside for him this long. Should he simply go out and see her? He didn't have the nerve, the official might come back at any moment. Bored, he looked at the lamp hanging from the ceiling. He took as long a run-up as he could, jumped and hit out at the lamp with his hand. It flew to one side, then swung to and fro. Reuben repeated this exercise several times, making the lamp swing violently. At the final blow the lead came away from the ceiling. The tin shade crashed into the wall with a loud clunk! and fell to the floor. Reuben was struck with panic. Immediately he regretted his foolish action that was sure to get him into trouble. A trickle of plaster was falling down from the place where the lamp had been suspended. The pieces grew bigger and bigger until there was a hole in the ceiling. Then, with a menacing screech, the leg of a desk appeared above, protruding into the room at an angle. At least it was something that would divert attention away from young Hecht as the cause of the damage.

And so it was that when the uniformed official returned a quarter of an hour later, she did not suspect Reuben. Ignoring the hole completely, she informed him, 'Reuben Hecht, you are assigned as official illustrator to the Research Institute dealing with the study of the aboriginals. This you owe to the fact that it was ordained by your father, who worked there as a hopeless case years ago. Major

Höfmeyer is willing to vouch for you. Here are your documents.'

How awful, he was going to be an official illustrator! And he was going to have to die some day as well . . .

He felt like flinging himself to the ground and howling until they offered him a life that was to his taste. For all his twisting and turning, he had still ended up precisely where his father had wanted him. *And* as an official illustrator. But he had no intention of going along with that. He'd rather be shot. He left the office with new, extremely vague thoughts of escape. What could he say to Edwina? And where was she anyway? He couldn't see her anywhere in the corridor. Perhaps she'd gone to the toilet? Not to reappear as a child, he hoped. Reuben stood there, unable to decide what to do. The angular official came out of her office.

'What are you doing hanging around here?' she bawled at him. 'Have you made a mess in your pants?'

'Where is my companion?' Reuben asked.

The answer was as follows:

'With your assignment to the Institute the question of guardianship is also settled once and for all. With immediate effect the Bureau, as the authority responsible for you, is your legal guardian, obviating the necessity for you to be accompanied by an adult. Therefore we have returned the lady to the frontier. She attached no importance to a personal farewell.'

And she had taken all the provisions with her!

Before Reuben could say anything, he was grasped by two of the Bureau's porters, greased and consigned to the pneumatic dispatch tube.

One hour after leaving the Bureau for the Assignment of Official Illustrators, Edwina reached the border post. Major Höfmeyer happened to be standing at the window, wondering whether there was any escape from the self and what the publisher might reply to his letter. He saw a patrol jeep drive up from which young Hecht's magnificent-looking companion descended. That could only mean one thing: she was leaving the Colony because the new-generation official illustrator had been successfully assigned to a position. And he, Höfmeyer, had made his own, modest contribution! He was happy to have been able to perform that belated service for his deceased friend. The father's work would live on in his son. The fortunate man had managed to find his way back to his origins and then, at the end, laboriously enough and full of remorse . . . and so on, and so on. It brought the odd tear to his eye.

The two border guards in the anteroom went wild when they saw Edwina again so soon. To impress her, they overturned furniture and peed on the suspension files. This, however, did not make the desired impression on the beautiful woman, merely brought them a disciplinary transfer. Major Höfmeyer issued Edwina's exit visa personally. With old-fashioned gallantry, he raised the barrier.

Once on the other side she immediately went to a telephone box. Höfmeyer dashed back into his office.

For security reasons he had the facility to listen in to conversations from that telephone.

Edwina rang her boss, Scherer-Dextry, telling him she was about to return. Sondergeld, she said, had employed a particularly sophisticated stratagem and was now in a position to continue on his own. He was operating under an assumed name and had managed to get himself a bona fide position as official illustrator. Scherer-Dextry expressed his delight at this, praising his young employee's enterprise and describing his scheme as brilliant. Edwina felt compelled to add, 'I would never have believed him capable of it. All the time I was with him he behaved like a complete idiot. Most ingenious, to say the least.'

'Amazing fellow!' roared Scherer-Dextry. 'He'll probably turn up in a couple of days with some milk-derived androids and the truth about Buckauer!'

Major Höfmeyer was following the conversation with the greatest of interest. 'The truth about Buckauer?' Quickly he got someone to check whom Edwina had been talking to.

The pneumatic dispatch system delivered Reuben to the State Institute for Primate Research, where they were attempting to uncover the secrets of the aboriginal population. Two of the Institute's porters received him, degreased him and took him to the Head of Personnel. Besides personnel matters, his responsibilities included above all the administration of the Institute's supplies of pencils, both lead and coloured. He remembered Lehmann Hecht very well, of course. He had heard rumours about the death of the distinguished anthropologist and offered young Hecht his condolences before going on to question him. Reuben told him about the eternal UHT-milk-drinking competitions, the complete fusion between his father and his bed, and his declared intention of hatching out a dwarf. Also that he had suddenly left his bed to pump air into the water-pipes. Out of respect for his father's memory, however, he omitted to mention the last thing he had heard him say as he left the house, namely that he would hang himself.

'Dreadful, dreadful,' said the Head of Personnel. 'Here, take a few pencils.'

With the pencils Reuben was to be sent to the department his father had belonged to. The porters were called in, regreased him and put him in the pneumatic dispatch tube. When he reached the Department he was welcomed, after having been degreased, by the head, Dr Sandel. However, she had no work for him.

'I'll be honest with you, Herr Hecht,' Dr Sandel said. 'Since your late father's time we have not been able to find out much at all about the aboriginal population. Here you can see a few drawings which indicate that the natives have fair complexions and blond hair. We suspect that both sexes have female characteristics. If there are actually two sexes then it will probably be the larger specimens that are the females.'

Reuben was surprised at this. 'Can't you just go and have a look?' he said.

'My dear young man,' Dr Sandel replied with a bitter smile, 'if only it were that simple! It's not that

we're not willing, oh no, but we just can't get anywhere near the natives. Neither with kindness, nor
with cunning, nor with brute force. Something completely new in the history of human colonisation! It
is only a question of time before their uncooperative
behaviour drives us out, mission unaccomplished.'
She lit a cigar. 'We have nothing concrete to go on,'
she continued, 'no artefacts, no bones, nothing. Not
even a few hairs . . .'

That was a word that triggered off associations in
Reuben's mind. Hair – blond – women: the hair in
the tin! The mysterious pallid blondes! Could they be
aboriginals from the Colony? Were they going round
the country of the occupying power causing may-
hem? Perhaps he had a pioneering contribution to
make to this area of research? In the name of science
he plucked up his courage, took out the tin and said,

'I have in here a blond hair that came into my
possession under mysterious circumstances. I have
grounds to believe it comes from creatures corresponding to the description you have just given.'

Dr Sandel stared wide-eyed at the hair in the cigarette tin.

'As you are Lehmann Hecht's son, I assume this is
not some kind of hoax,' she said severely. 'I will
therefore institute an immediate and thorough
investigation of this hair. Follow me.'

They set off at the double for a particular laboratory. In it was a huge machine just waiting to be
finally put into service. Right next to the main
switch was a label saying, *When are you finally
going to put me into service?* Dr Sandel operated the

complex monster as surely as if it were nothing more than a photocopying machine. Conscious that he might be about to witness, indeed to have brought about, a scientific breakthrough, Reuben was rather excited as he looked on. Had something his father had striven for years to achieve simply fallen into his lap, so to speak? He watched with mounting tension as the hair was inserted into the machine in a very precise way. All sorts of buttons were pressed, here and there lights went on. After a few minutes the results were disgorged in the form of long rows of lines and squiggles. Dr Sandel counted the chromosomes, frowning and eventually shaking her head.

'Unfortunately not,' she said. 'It doesn't come from the aboriginal population, that is one hundred per cent certain. It's not a normal human hair either, though.'

'But?' asked Reuben, devastated.

Dr Sandel handed the hair back to him. 'An android hair. Androids derived from milk have that kind of hair.'

The thoughts and feelings this answer sparked off in the young man do not need to be described in detail. The shock was too great. The tip of his shoe, that he had stuck back on last Saturday during his journey to the concert, fell off again. With a groan, Reuben took his tube of 'Dr Wirefather's Special Glue for Broken-off Shoe-tips' out of his side pocket and repaired the damage.

'Where did you get this hair?' asked Dr Sandel.

Without mentioning the exact spot where he found it, Reuben told her everything he knew. Dr

Sandel listened, but said nothing. Reuben was convinced he had a right to the truth about these androids. He patted his jacket[1] on the place where the tin with the hair was back in his inside pocket and demanded an explanation.

As the son of the late Lehmann Hecht, he was entitled to one, Dr Sandel accepted that. She lit a new cigar, the previous one having been forgotten somewhere.

'Let's go back to my office,' she suggested. 'I'll give you a piggyback, if you like.'

That was an offer he could not possibly accept. In a sudden fit of gallantry, he insisted that she ride on his back. And she did. Whether it was a cunning ploy on the part of an older, more experienced woman who had the advantage of an academic education, or whether it simply happened like that, is something we would not presume to say.

When they reached the office, she dismounted and offered Reuben a seat in a sumptuous leather armchair. She sat at her desk, and smoked and talked. Reuben learnt that his father, irritated by the refusal of the aboriginals to conform to the demands of scientific research, had conducted some peculiar experiments. Partly to occupy his time and partly to work off the aforementioned irritation, he started making homunculi. In this venture he had to get round the ban on creating artificial humans from, as you might put it, flesh and blood. He tried this and

---

[1] Gronius and Rauschenbach would have formulated it thus: 'He thwacked his leather jerkin.'

that, including petrol and silicon, but none of the results were satisfactory. The petrol-silicon beings, for example, had strange fringes with tufts of ermine and had to drag their buttocks along the ground behind them. Experiments with tofu were equally disappointing. It was using UHT milk as a basis that Lehmann Hecht finally succeeded in producing worthwhile creatures. As far as their appearance was concerned, he modelled them on the available portraits of aboriginals. With infinite patience – and not a few wily tricks – he finally managed to produce four remarkably convincing androids which could not be distinguished from living people. That was the time when his addiction to UHT milk began. He became a terminally hopeless case. Naturally the Institute for Primate Research was anything but delighted at this turn of events. Androids from milk were not what had been ordered, consequently Hecht's research grant was withdrawn and he was required to eliminate his homunculi and leave the Colony. At home legal proceedings for the misappropriation of research funds awaited him.

It didn't come to the extermination of the androids, as they had long since made themselves scarce. They were of a boisterous disposition, which from the very start had made it totally impossible for the anthropologist to keep them under control. Alongside their teenage rebelliousness, they developed certain supernatural powers and were soon more than their creator could cope with. Lehmann Hecht intensified his consumption of UHT milk in an attempt to counter this, but it made no impression on them whatsoever. As bold as brass, they declared that, since he had brought them into the world, he was responsible for their welfare and upkeep. As matters came to a head and it would not be long before the Institute demanded their elimination, they used Hecht's milk-conversion technology to fabricate an escape vehicle. It was assumed they had gone even before Lehmann Hecht left the Colony. Naturally this was hushed up by the State Institute for Primate Research.

Reuben could hardly believe his ears. His own father was responsible for the existence of those pallid blondes! And what a fool they'd made of him, persuading him they were the Flesh-eating Fetish Bitches. But, just a minute – wasn't that who they were? There *had* been four blond women on the stage . . . What could they want from him? Had they singled him out because of some kind of family feeling? It couldn't be a question of the often-quoted 'call of the blood', since it was presumably milk circulating in their veins. Nevertheless, it couldn't be pure chance that they kept on running into him of all people. There must be something specific behind it, but what?

The regulations required Dr Sandel to make an official report of the contact between Reuben and the escaped androids. It was certain that he would have to appear before a committee of inquiry. First of all, however, he had to be found a place to work and to sleep. To this end, he was stamped and, after a brief farewell from Dr Sandel, returned to the Head of Personnel.

The Head of Personnel stared at the palms of his hands for a long time, then finally said, 'I've got something here! This is something for you. A scientist who is investigating the cremation rites of the local seals. Liliencron's the man's name. You can even stay with him. That would mean you wouldn't have to live in a hostel like so many official painters and illustrators who have no home of their own in the Colony.'

He made out a transfer order, which Reuben would have to give to the scientist. However, because of the uncertain state of security in the Colony since the Worldchild and Kneerider incident, Reuben's departure was delayed. The place where he would be working was several days' journey away on the remotest edge of the Colony. It would take a whole week, the Head of Personnel told him, before an escort could be assembled and would venture out. Until then, he went on, Reuben would have to make do with the hostel for unmarried official painters and illustrators.

'You must stay in the hostel until your escort comes to collect you. Until then you are on what we might call compassionate leave. Perhaps you could practise drawing Colony seals?'

Reuben did not answer. He wasn't going to draw anything, ever again. He would absolutely refuse to do any drawing at all, he had made up his mind about that and he would stick by it, even if they shot him. But whether he wanted to or no, he had to go to the hostel. That was the only alternative to the ear-splitting noise that greeted him out in the street. He set off at a trot to get inside the hostel as quickly as possible.

With no luggage and forebodings of disaster, he followed the route described by the Head of Personnel, his hands pressed tight against his ears. Only that morning he had set off, happy as a lark, in the company of an extremely attractive woman, to spend an indefinite period holed up at Worldchild and Kneerider's. 'Huh, Worldchild and Kneerider, those two wallies,' the words of the electric Archqueen came back to mind. How right she had been! Just because of some private problems 'those two wallies' must have had with the aboriginals at the very moment when he was going to see them, he had been deprived of Edwina's presence and forced to go and stay in the hostel for unmarried illustrators. He viewed his proposed stay with Worldchild and Kneerider, whom, of course he didn't know, through rose-tinted spectacles, insisting on seeing it as a kind of Golden Age, even though it was far from certain he would have stayed with them at all. He pictured to himself how they would have admired and envied him, turning up with such a fantastic woman. He would have spent the whole livelong day being envied, looking at Edwina and drinking rum. He would have known nothing of his father's responsibility for the four pallid blondes, because he would not have met Dr Sandel. And he would have avoided all that greasing and degreasing.

His imaginings suddenly took a less agreeable turn when the thought occurred to him that Edwina would certainly have mentioned their commission for

Scherer-Dextry, at which Worldchild and Kneerider would have talked of nothing but androids derived from milk. Perhaps they wouldn't have admired and envied him at all, but locked him up in the broom cupboard and fawned on Edwina. At once he removed his rose-tinted spectacles. No matter how he looked at it, he was stuck in an impossible situation with no future. And the next hassles were already being lined up: his interrogation by the commission of inquiry because of his contact with the escaped androids – androids who owed their existence to his father – then prosecution for refusal to work, followed by an inevitable guilty verdict. Prior to that, the conditions in the hostel would doubtless do their part in wearing him down.

'And I'm going to have to die some day as well,' he remembered. He would have liked to curse his fate roundly, knee it in the groin and give it a good thrashing. Instead he had to enter the hostel, a stupid, warped box made of concrete slabs. The hall was dominated by faded wallpaper of the worst kind and the maniacal laughter of bloated people (probably suffering from venereal disease). Reuben elbowed his way to the reception desk. There was the warden, worrying about fictitious ivy roots which might one day get so thick they would lift up the concrete slabs. His wife had taken to her bed weeks ago and could not sleep for horrific visions of Virginia creeper getting into the hostel chimney and making everything explode. For that reason any plant growth in the hostel, however tentative, was rigourously extirpated.

Reluctantly Reuben announced his arrival. The Head of Personnel had indeed sent notification. The warden went on and on at him in sentences that were confused and fundamentally incomplete.

'How fortunate are all those who don't have to go through this here and now,' thought Reuben. 'I wonder if they have rum here? You need to be drunk all day.'

Because he was receiving special treatment and on compassionate leave, he was given a single room. It was at the end of a corridor stuffed full of horrible busts and no bigger than a one-horse carriage. It contained the chair in which Goethe died and a bath-tub with no lock. In one corner was something vaguely mattress-shaped. Or was it a soldier rolled flat by tanks? No, just a mattress that had been disembowelled, or perhaps exploded by a Virginia creeper. There were no towels, no soap, nothing. All Reuben had with him were the clothes he stood up in. The amenities left much to be desired and it was no use expecting anything from the warden as that kind of thing was a matter for the residents alone. Instead, the new arrival had been most strongly urged not to miss the informal get-together celebrated in the cellar every evening. Reuben had not the slightest intention of exposing himself to the company of graphical riff-raff and their coarse language. He stayed in his room, not eating or drinking, only using the lavatory. The mattress was so disgusting he spent the night in Goethe's death-chair.

Nor did he appear at the communal breakfast table next morning. Around midday he was thrown out for contravening hostel regulations. What now? Go back and pester the Head of Personnel with an account of his case, which would be reported to him anyway? Submit to a dressing-down for his behaviour? Perhaps even be summoned to appear before another committee of inquiry? Not an attractive prospect.

It would be better to start an affair with the under-age daughter of a senior official illustrator. On the notice-board of the hostel for unmarried illustrators and painters were various lonely-hearts ads secretly pinned up by young ladies. Reuben studied them before leaving the building. One was interesting:

Iconoclast female (17)
WLTM tolerant male illustration-refusenik, (Distance Learning Academy Defector welcome), with view to mutual excesses.
Interests: music, dance, French horn . . .
Grete Landolfi, Tel . . .

'She's looking for *me*,' thought Reuben. He pocketed the notice, stole some change from the warden and went to the nearest telephone box. As he was about to dial, his call to the Flesh-eating Fetish Bitches' fan club came to mind. That must have been the last time he spoke to a woman on the phone. He scrolled through the memory then dialled Grete Landolfi's number. For the first time he heard the ringing tone used in the Colony, an exact copy of the one at home. They had obviously deliberately avoided an alternative signal, on the one hand to make people in the Colony feel at home and on the other to avert any separatist developments after the American model of 1776.

Grete Landolfi answered, her voice easily distinguishable from the ringing tone. Using the appropriate expressions, Reuben applied for the position advertised. Since he assured her that he possessed all the required qualifications, he was invited to an immediate interview.

He had neither eaten nor slept for thirty hours. He hoped he would be able to make up for the loss of food and sleep at Grete Landolfi's house, assuming he didn't collapse in a heap, as he had done twenty years ago in Abidjan, and wake up at home in bed.

It was a long way from the hostel to the Landolfi villa and on the way he felt as if he were being pushed in a wheelchair by a bearded man in a diving suit. At least Rossman and Prümers didn't appear. Reuben was completely wrapped up in visions of eating and drinking, washing, cleaning his teeth and stretching his body out in a horizontal position. Exhausted as he was, the Parasumi noise outside was the final straw. He promptly collapsed in a heap. That is, he fell over together with the wheelchair in which he was sitting. The bearded man in the diving suit righted both it and him.

'All bad things come to an end,' he said. 'Here is the Landolfi villa.'

He tried to rub brilliantine into Reuben's hair. Reuben, warding him off with his last ounces of strength, saw that the house of Senior Official

Illustrator Landolfi was a definite eyesore among the surrounding villas in the Colonial style, some of which were truly magnificent. The Landolfi house was completely without architectural charm, grey, dilapidated, almost a ruin.

The man and the wheelchair had vanished. Reuben pressed the bell beside which, carved into the rock, was LANDOLFI, SENIOR OFFICIAL ILLUSTRATOR. He heard a crash inside the house, then steps approaching the door. The relentless Parasumi din filled the air. The door opened to reveal a young woman.

She looked the way she ought to, and seemed to do what she could to achieve the effect she wanted. The words of the poet came into Reuben's mind: 'She is the magnificent abode . . . she is the armoured flower of lustful eyes . . . she is the seventh breast of the moon goddess . . .' Producing the lonely-hearts ad, he told her he was the one who had just phoned.

'Would you mind coming back to the table,' barked a male voice from the depths of the house.

Grete explained that the family were just having lunch. To make a good impression, Reuben said nothing about how hungry he was. He was taken upstairs, to Grete's room, where she told him to stay until she came back from lunch. The room consisted mainly of bedding, items of clothing strewn all around the place and cosmetics. No comparison with his cubbyhole in the hostel. There were no pictures to be seen, but then this was where an iconoclast had her abode. Reuben lay down on the mattress and fell asleep straightaway. He dreamt of something, but couldn't quite make out what. Perhaps something beginning with a K or a P. When he woke up it was early evening. Grete was sitting opposite him.

'Oh God, how embarrassing,' he stammered. 'A total stranger comes to the house for the first time and immediately goes to sleep for hours . . .'

By now it was time for Grete to go back downstairs for dinner. Reuben had to wait again. Herr Landolfi would never have put up with any Tom, Dick or Harry coming to eat at his table. And had he had the slightest suspicion the person concerned was a deserter, he would have informed the authorities on the spot. Fortunately the suspicion never occurred to him.

Half an hour later Grete returned with the left-overs from dinner. However, after a thirty-seven-and-a-half-hour fast, they were not enough to satisfy Reuben, and Grete had to go back down to the kitchen and steal a loaf of bread and three tins of sardines. Had he had a wooden leg, Reuben would have carved three notches in it when he had finished, one for each tin. And Grete would have been astonished at the number of notches in it already. 'Wow, it won't be long before it snaps,' she would have said. As it was, he carved them in the table Grete had found that someone had put out for rubbish. Then he added all the other notches, for all the tins of sardines he had ever consumed. As he carved he told her about himself.

Grete was impressed. Reuben fulfilled all the pre-requisites perfectly. What she didn't tell him was that he was the only one who had responded to her notice. There were not many illustration drop-outs since the career prospects were very good. Grete hated drawing and everything associated with it. Her father, as an official illustrator, demanded in a pedagogically ham-fisted manner that his children follow in his footsteps. His daughter absolutely refused and his son had had a breakdown because of the pressure from his father. Grete had alarming things to tell about her brother. He was completely mad, she said, was already wearing a girdle and was sure to kill himself soon.

Reuben found that regrettable. After his refreshing sleep and nourishing sustenance he felt like a new man, or at least a new teenager. There were even a few tots of rum siphoned off from Herr Landolfi's drinks cabinet. Then his hostess invited him to smoke a wad of Colony grass with her in her French horn. Before starting, he insisted she give him written assurance that it wouldn't make him addicted. Although it made Reuben cough quite a lot, he resolutely inhaled the smoke with its comfy aroma.

A French horn will take a fair amount, and afterwards Grete thought her name was Esakidiodë. Reuben waxed eloquent in laying down an extended formulation of the history of mankind based on a new kind of inference.[2] In this extended formulation, the direct logical conclusion represented a special

[2] Developed at the same time by a certain Leistikov, who praised it to the skies in an effort to offload it onto all sorts of publishing houses.

case which was extended by the a) 'directly similar' and b) 'indirectly similar' conclusion. Thanks to this new kind of inference, his universal formula was capable of explaining *everything*, in contrast to those that are non-self-validating because they are based solely on direct logic. That opened up the possibility of an entirely new interpretation of the concept of the deity. Furthermore, he could even name the 'causes and individual ratings of the so-called mental illnesses' and break down drug abuse according to the reasons for the specific action of all drugs, which he was able to cite completely without recourse to specialist jargon.

When at last he felt himself fully ready for the act of coition, Reuben found there was a surprise in store for him. Not only did his body suddenly lack all male characteristics, it corresponded in every detail to that of a well-developed seventeen-year-old girl. In that situation, how could he hope to practise reasonable sex with Grete? She explained with a giggle that the change was brought about by the Colony grass.

'The aboriginals smoke the stuff all day, with the result that the men and women converge anatomically.'

'Oh yes.' Now Reuben remembered. 'Among the aboriginals both sexes look like women. Applying my method of extended formulation, the *similar inference* leads me to the following result: because of their respective roles within the development of the species, the two sexes live in different time zones. Smoking the Colony grass abolishes that factor and the time differential disappears. Interesting that the convergence should take place on the female level and not the male.'

He wondered whether Dr Sandel knew anything about this. Shouldn't he inform her? But all this theory was quickly pushed into the background by a more pressing, practical question: given the situation, how was he going to practise reasonable sex with Grete?

'Why on earth did you do that?' he asked her. It turned out that it wasn't out of thoughtlessness, malice or to promote homosexual activities. Being a minor, she said, her father would not allow her over-night visits from males. If Reuben was to stay the night despite the ban, he would have to smoke a suf-ficient dose of Colony grass for the effeminisation to last until morning. Before they went to bed he would have to be presented to her father for inspection.

They went to his study. The senior official illus-trator carried out a dispassionate examination of Reuben's anatomy and, after merely sketching the taking of a blood sample with his pencil sharpener, granted his permission. Reuben jumped through this bureaucratic hoop with aplomb and composure. After all, when you looked at it closely, it wasn't his own private parts he was showing to a complete stranger. And anyway, it was still better than hostels, committees of inquiry or homelessness. With a brusque command, the pipe-smoking, arrogant bastard of a senior official illustrator ordered the two girls out of his study, but not before they had to listen to a monologue which amply demonstrated his qualification for several thousand of the best.

'My self-spiritual intimate conscience is my inner truth. Without ceasing, my intimate self-feeling is indomitably active within me; on a spiritual-organic level I am bio-psychogenetically self-predetermined. Only I alone, through myself alone, do *everything* absolutely right. All other people do everything completely wrong, their activities are pointless.[3] And now piss off.'

Going back up the stairs, Grete asked Reuben if he was prepared to kill her father. He promised to think about it. Later on he lay there in the dark, unable to sleep. He had caught up on his sleep not all that long ago and his unaccustomed female body kept him awake. It was only towards five o'clock that wakefulness went its own way. When he woke up in the morning, desperate for a pee, his old familiar urogenital state of affairs had been restored.

During the day the two young people abandoned themselves to mutual excesses. At night Reuben stayed with Grete as a young woman and every evening he put up with the bureaucratic check on his intake of Colony grass and the patriarch's monologue. For weeks on end.

He also got to know the brother, a broken man, driven over the edge of madness by his father. Grinning like a cockeyed nutcracker, the poor devil declared he was a forest Indian. Not a spare-time Indian, oh no! More and more he felt himself to be a forest Indian, he said.

---

[3] With these words Landolfi also shows himself to be a follower of the 'EGO-man' of Braunlage.

'Forest Indians need money, but they refuse to accept any.'

As such he wanted to live wild and free, he went on, that was what he had been born for, the forest was his home.

'The forest is the refuge of the German soul!' A forest Indian with a German soul! The seed planted by Karl May had borne fruit! Reginald – that was the unfortunate young man's name – demanded 'a return to our roots, to our old folk values, our old religion, to our old gods and goddesses, our spirits, sprites and fairies, our runes, rites and rituals.' Moreover he had produced, he told Reuben, about thirty-five poems, mostly on political themes, poems of a kind Reginald claimed never to have come across anywhere else. He had already offered them to an old-established Leipzig publishing house, he proudly announced. Although it was his wish to see these poems all published together in a book of normal format, he realised no publisher would be willing to take on such a risky enterprise, if only because of the threat of terrorist action, which had to be reckoned with, given the subject matter. But he wouldn't want to publish the book at his own cost. He would prefer, he said, to have no expenses and pocket the royalties. Reuben just kept on nodding. Then Reginald lost his composure and wanted to know what was to be done if, 'contrary to expectation, a potential pub-lisher should bring personal responsibility into the reckoning?' He finally left, foaming at the mouth.

About two weeks later Reuben was alone in Grete's room reading Louis Flamel's *The Lascivious*

Sponges. The Landolfi family was gathered round the supper table. Suddenly the reading lamp went off and the radio, which had been playing music by the Flesh-eating Fetish Bitches, fell silent. Uttering a few choice swear-words, Reuben got up to check the fuse box. To do that, he had to leave the room. On the gloomy landing he became aware of a loud roaring and crackling. He stood still, like a beast at pasture. The noise, which sounded very inappropriate, was definitely coming from the direction of Reginald's room. Automatically he went closer. At the door a considerable temperature could be detected. From the other side came an uninhibited sizzling sound. Well brought up as he was, Reuben knocked first. When no one answered, he opened the door. Raging flames leapt out towards him, the heat was unbearable. Hurriedly he closed the door.

So Reginald had set fire to his room. Obviously the blaze had caused a short circuit, but presumably only in the upstairs supply. No one downstairs seemed to have noticed it yet. Reuben could not help feeling it would be appropriate to go downstairs and inform them. That, however, was not unproblematic. His attendance at meals had been expressly forbidden, and if he appeared nevertheless, and with such an announcement, it was hardly likely to endear him to the head of the family. On the other hand, he couldn't really wait until the whole house was burning and the family found out for themselves. He was sure to be asked why he had not noticed anything and warned the others. With a sigh, he made his way down to the ground floor. He went into the dining-room and said, in as matter-of-fact, unassuming and polite tones as possible,

'Excuse me, I don't want to be a nuisance, but everything's going up in flames upstairs.'

Father, mother and daughter gave shrill squawks and, in a reflex action, threw their plates and cutlery at the ceiling. Reginald, who was also at the table, appeared not to understand what was going on but instinctively joined in the squawking. The family charged out through the door, knocking Reuben to the ground. Oddly enough, they got the fire under control very quickly, probably because the forest Indian's room was already completely burnt out. Later, in the gap between the obligatory anatomical check and the monologue, Senior Official Illustrator Landolfi said to Reuben that all good deeds reaped their just reward and handed him a twenty mark note.

VI

In Brunswick the director of the Academy, Mothor-heym, was spitting at the wall. For weeks now no new drawings had come from Reuben Hecht and the monthly payments from his parents had failed to arrive for the second time. The publisher who was going to bring out his uncouth handbook of medicine had sent a letter which amounted to an ultimatum. Twenty years was enough to produce such a handbook, he wrote. He described the way he had been willing to wait as truly courageous, but now his patience was at an end. He had a board of directors breathing down his neck, he continued, who regularly cast an eye over the stocks and were asking awkward questions about why an uncouth handbook of medicine needed such a long gestation period. The board, he went on, clearly favoured other projects, which were of greater interest for the firm, slim editions of verse, for example, and above all exclusive books of animal fables with applied poetry, all small volumes with a big future. They would publish them with an initial run of 35,000 and give away a bicycle with every book. If the manuscript of the medical handbook was not ready within the next three months, the project would fall victim to an 'emergency cull' designed to remove dead wood from the system.

Mothorheym addressed a few choice epithets to the absent publisher then dashed into the secretariat

181

of the Holy German Paintbrush Distance Learning Academy.

'What's going on with that bloody Hecht?' he shouted. 'Why's he not sending any drawings? Why haven't we received any payments?'

Only now did he hear about the call from the Bureau for the Assignment of Official Illustrators and the request for written confirmation of Reuben Hecht's status as a student. Mothorheym himself had signed the letter without giving it a further thought.

'The Bureau for the Assignment of Official Illustrators?!' he screamed. 'But that's in Neu-Worpswede! Does that mean our student is in the Colony?'

He recalled Reuben Hecht's flight to the Ivory Coast twenty years previously. 'Once a defector, always a defector!'

Immediately he telephoned the Bureau in the Colony. There he learnt that Reuben Hecht had initially been assigned to the State Institute for Primate Research, but then detailed to assist a scientist who was carrying out research into the cremation rites of seals. He had been allocated temporary accommodation in the hostel for unmarried illustrators, from which he had gone absent without leave. He was still at large.

Again and again the director of the Academy stamped his foot and spat at the wall. In his fury, he tidied up his desk; he was so furious, he could have cleaned the windows. Then, underneath weeks of old files, he found a newspaper cutting clipped to a note: the article in the Brunswick local paper on the death of the distinguished anthropologist, Lehmann Hecht. Mothorheym spent the rest of the working day cleaning windows.

He had an important phone call to make, but caution suggested he make it from his private number. He hurried home and pushed aside his wife, who was wearing a dress that was far too short. It was fear driving him, fear produced by an over-burdened conscience. Once in his soundproofed study he dialled the number of his henchmen in the Colony, Worldchild and Kneerider. They were the ones he entrusted with the task of looking after his interests out there, most recently in the case of Sondergeld. The only thing that troubled him was that he could not monitor their activities. True, they reported every time that his instructions had been successfully carried out, but they never actually supplied any proof. Mothorheym, having no means of checking up, was compelled to believe and trust them.

It was a very bad line. During the noise months telephone connections with the Colony were subject to severe disruption. By now, however, the cold season had begun, yet the connection was still very poor. A soft, squeaky voice replied. Mothorheym could not understand a thing. He asked whether that was Worldchild and Kneerider's number, and the voice answered yes.

'Speak up!' he shouted down the receiver. 'It's a lousy connection. Can you hear me?'

There was an answer which sounded something like 'no time' and 'psychological tests'. Mothorheym could restrain himself no longer and bellowed his question into the receiver. The moment he mentioned the name Reuben Hecht, the voice at the other end started wailing and repeating the name in a tone of dumbfounded enquiry.

'Yes, Reuben Hecht,' Mothorheym confirmed. 'He's been in the Colony for the last few weeks.'

A tumult broke out at the other end. Now there were two voices screeching and squawking. It even sounded as if an iron snow-shovel were being scraped across the receiver. Mothorheym kept shouting 'Hey there!' and 'Now just listen!' for several minutes until things calmed down. He was wondering what could have got into Worldchild and Kneerider. When it seemed that what he said would actually be understood, he gave them the order to capture Reuben Hecht and bring him to Brunswick as quickly as possible. His intention, of course, was to compel Reuben to complete the missing drawings for the medical handbook during the next three months. After that his plan was to have him committed to Frau Suse's clinic, where he assumed Sondergeld already was. The two voices bawled, 'Cursèd be Reuben Hecht!' and swore a fervent oath not to rest until they had captured the fugitive. Then they seemed to simply drop the receiver and dash off at once. Somewhat mystified, the director of the Academy rang off. Immediately he was filled with impatience for Worldchild and Kneerider's report of 'Mission accomplished!'

The next morning he received a letter from the publishers. It said they were definitely cancelling the medical handbook. After waiting for twenty years, the board had lost both their patience and all interest. The editor's decision was final. This demanded more than just spitting at the wall. Mothorheym felt he had been cheated out of twenty irreplaceable years and out of the crowning glory of his career. He might just as well have died twenty years ago. He was literally sizzling with pain and fury. Any moment now he might start smouldering or turning cartwheels all the way to Schweinfurth. The time had come to write a blunt letter to that swine of a publisher, wrap it round a brick and heave it through the appropriate window. Mothorheym wrote:

Sir!

After twenty years of preparation, so close to the completion of my life's work, you have the audacity to do this to me!? To pander obsequiously to the niggling petty-mindedness of a board of directors who are philistines to a man, to sacrifice unhesitatingly a major publishing project, one that has been decades in the making, on the altar of short-sighted commercial interest!? Shame on you, sir, shame! This 'reaction' is NOT, I repeat, NOT what I would have expected from a firm such as yours. Has the editorial board been abolished? Am I not right in thinking you are an old-established Leipzig publishing house? Do you think I can afford to consign years of my life and work to the scrap heap? Just like that? Wasted effort?

Oleam et operam perdidi! If you have any idea what that means.

185

I do NOT remain, sir,
your obedient servant

> *Mothorheym*
> *(Director,*
> *Holy German Paintbrush*
> *Distance Learning Academy)*

The next thing was to modify his orders to World-child and Kneerider. It was no longer necessary for Reuben Hecht to produce further drawings. However, they had to ensure that he didn't by some unfortunate chance learn certain things, as that Sondergeld had done before him. It was unlikely, but one had to expect the unexpected.

Mothorheym was worried he wouldn't be able to contact Worldchild and Kneerider. There had been something definitive about the way they had left the previous day. However, someone did answer. Another unknown voice could be heard through the crackling and hissing. Again he was assured he had the right number.

'I'm glad I managed to get you,' said Mothorheym. The voice replied with a sentence containing the words 'back', 'write a letter' and 'publishers'. Speaking in a loud, clear voice, Mothorheym explained the change in orders. 'Reuben Hecht is to be taken without delay to the Colony branch of Frau Suse's clinic.'

Again hysterical shouting and the sound of people disappearing at the double was to be heard. Mothorheym replaced the receiver. It irked him to be dependent on these lunatics without being able to check up on them.

VII

After the fire in Reginald's bedroom, Landolfi had had his son scrapped. On the deregistration form he ticked 'shut-down, . . . b) permanent'. Frau Landolfi had also disappeared. She had been sold ('slightly foxed, some rubbing, spine a little faded and reinforced with sellotape, corners bumped, edges slightly chipped, otherwise VG'). It had not yet been finally settled which poor bastard would have to do all the essential housework, but it looked very much as if Grete was going to get stuck with it.

One Wednesday afternoon Landolfi came home from work earlier than usual. Instead of disappearing into his study, he stormed up the stairs and kicked down the door to Grete's room, which was locked, bellowing, 'Where's the blighter who's been living in my house, sponging off me for weeks?'

Grete made bold to ask what he thought he was doing but was knocked to the floor with a hefty box round the ears. Reuben took fright, not only in view of the physical violence already dealt out and still to come, but also because Landolfi could report him to the authorities. And that was just what the 'EGO-man' had in mind. During his lunch break he had read a biased account of Reuben's case in *Official Illustration Weekly*. It made his hair sit up and beg when the pfennig dropped and he realised that it was he, of all people, who had been sheltering this deserter.

'Name?' bawled Landolfi at Reuben. 'Tell me your name at once and show me your ID.'

He gave Grete a preventative box round the ears, but she simply hadn't the nerve to stab the martinet with the nearest pointed object. Reuben muttered that he was called Aaron von Bitschesflesch and had lost his papers. Beside himself with rage, Landolfi pushed him in the chest and roared, 'A liar into the bargain! I'll tell you what you're called. You're called Reuben Hecht! It's all here in black and white.'

And with that he stuck the *Official Illustration Weekly* under Reuben's nose. They had even printed a full-page photograph of the wanted youth, though reversed, as could be seen from the parting and the mouth, which looked somehow warped.

'The game is up,' Landolfi went on. 'I am going to hand you over to the authorities immediately. First of all, however, we must settle our accounts. Thirty-five days you've spent under my roof, thus obtaining thirty-five times three meals by fraudulent means. If we deduct one day – corresponding to the 20.00 DM you received as a reward – that still leaves thirty-four times three, that is one hundred and two meals. Have you sufficient money to cover that? I thought not. The debt will be collected in a thrashing corresponding to the sum due.'

He silenced his protesting daughter with a technical knock-out. Now it was Reuben's turn. However, one second before the furious lunatic could get his hands on his victim, who was backing away in alarm, the air was suddenly rent with a noise like the sound of a centrifugal pump. Something dark and indefinable which, one moment later, wasn't there any more, seemed to be aimed directly at the frenzied unfortunate. He was disabled and dismantled, disconnected, disarticulated, disassembled and totally destroyed. The only thing left of him was a few crumbs of what looked like charcoal and some particles of soot.

'Serves him right, the stupid bogeyman,' said Grete, rubbing her head, which was still ringing from the three right hooks her father had landed. The Landolfi household was a thing of the past.

'I'm going away,' declared Grete. 'A human being should have no household.'

Reuben completed her declaration. 'Instead, a human being should drink schnapps from dawn till dusk.'

Grete intended to join a revolutionary cell of iconoclasts, if necessary to found one. Farther to the north, on the edge of the Neu-Worpswede marshes, there was supposed to be a colony of neo-ikonoborzic illustration refuseniks. Reuben could not be persuaded to join them.

'Okay. Then we'll just have to go our separate ways,' said Grete. As far as the contents of the house were concerned, her suggestion was, 'Let's take what we need and can carry. The rest we'll burn.'

So they sorted out any items they could use: the contents of her father's drinks cabinet, plenty of provisions, ready cash, changes of underwear. In the senior official illustrator's study Grete contemplated a row of box-files on a shelf. 'I'm against loading myself up with too much, but *those* are certainly not staying here,' she said.

Reuben asked what they were and was told, 'My father's blackmail files. He archived highly embarrassing documents concerning as many prominent members of the illustration profession as possible and blackmailed them. These files are as good as ready cash. They'll secure my financial future.'

'So you going to continue the blackmail?'

'Yes. It's my inheritance. I'll set things in motion as soon as I've found somewhere to stay.'

'She's all right,' thought Reuben, 'she's provided for. But what about me? All I've got to look forward to is a life on the run with a great deal of hassle. Perhaps I should stay with her after all? She's a good catch now and she is the one I had the first sexual intercourse of my life with . . .'

While he was thinking, he suddenly noticed something. On the back of one of the box-files was the name 'Mothorheym'.

The director of the Holy German Paintbrush Distance Learning Academy! So Landolfi had been blackmailing *him*? What with? What can he have found out about him?

Grete went upstairs to find a suitcase that would take all thirty-seven box-files, enough time for Reuben to study the Mothorheym papers. The material they contained was highly explosive! Reuben was so astounded he almost sprouted a pair of antlers. Landolfi's extensive notes allowed him to reconstruct a quite outrageous case, the Mothorheym scandal. The documents also revealed

how Landolfi had come into possession of the information. As a professional blackmailer he naturally
had all the specialist sources at his disposal. In this
particular case Worldchild and Kneerider, the agents
for anything and everything who had probably been
kidnapped by the aboriginals, had been his suppliers.

'Well, well, well,' thought Reuben, 'those fishy
gentlemen again. Everyone seems to have had
doings with them. Even the late, unlamented senior
official illustrator with his self-spiritual intimate
conscience.'

The files were so meticulously kept that even at
the speed at which he was forced to read them
Reuben had no problem working out the following:

At a certain point in the past a young illustrator
had left the Colonial Service. The reason he gave for
this change of career was that he had found a lucra-
tive source of income outside the Colony, i.e. in the
homeland. The nature of this source remained
unknown to the authorities, but not to Worldchild
and Kneerider. They, who poked their noses and their
fingers into every pie in the Colony, had received
information to the effect that the young man had
specialised in copying Buckauer's style and had done
it to such effect that he had been very successful. The
files also revealed how he had come into contact with
Buckauer's drawings. In some poorly produced children's books he had discovered illustrations signed
with the name Buckauer and had been captivated
once and for all by their perverted charm. They were
so indescribably singular that they continued to
haunt him until he felt under a compulsion to copy

the style. Reuben could not believe that anyone would become involved with this kind of material of their own volition. But then people did all kinds of strange things, didn't they? And there were people who collected the stuff, as he had seen with Scherer-Dextry. Clearly the manager of the freak show was not the only connoisseur of that style, there must be a number of people prepared to fork out a lot of money for Buckauer's drawings. Back home the young ex-official illustrator, who was making a good living from the sale of Buckauer forgeries, gradually started to feel the need to find out everything about his idol and if possible even to get to know him personally. That, however, had turned out to be problematic since, as Scherer-Dextry had already complained to Reuben, nothing was known about the artist. The young forger started to get desperate. Not desperate enough to sift through the telephone directories of every town and region, the personnel files of the army, the merchant navy and the voluntary fire-brigades, police records, newspaper archives, death registers, it is true, but he did put an 'information wanted' advert in specialist journals that were read both at home and in the Colony. He received one reply, from a Frau Gotz-Goldstein in the Colony. He travelled there to see her and she explained the facts of Buckauer to him. To his surprise, Frau Gotz-Goldstein started off by describing the early career of a quite different man, a man by the name of – Mothorheym. This name was naturally familiar to the ex-official illustrator, since he had been trained at the Holy German Paintbrush Distance Learning

Academy and the director at the time had been none other than Professor Mothorheym. The latter's early career was, however, entirely unexpected.

CAREER OF MOTHORHEYM – SOURCE: WORLDCHILD & KNEERIDER

In his youth strongly attracted to art. Parents thought M lacked talent, demanded do apprenticeship in commercial undertaking. M secretly applied for place at well-known art school with a few wild scrawls. Rejected. Threw himself on floor in secretary's office and screamed didn't want to go into commerce. Professor by name of Gotz-Goldstein felt sorry for him, let him carry her keys and sometimes even open up the life-drawing classroom or various cupboards. Although G-G thought drawings M produced with increasing enthusiasm repulsive, out of kindness of heart found number of small commissions for illustration (books for young people, adventure books, Wild West literature). By means of various dirty tricks (targeted intrigues, character assassination, bribery, threats of violence, see attached documents) M soon made professor, later even director of Holy German Paintbrush Distance Learning Academy in Brunswick. M's lawyer managed to get all proceedings instituted against him dismissed. Professor G-G compelled to flee to Colony because would have been prepared to testify against M. M's greatest fear: G-G only one who knows young M used pseudonym 'Buckauer' for drawings.

The Buckauer forger's hair had stood on end (as had Reuben's on reading the notes) when Professor Gotz-Goldstein showed him all kinds of proofs demonstrating Mothorheym's culpability, and which would have made him a social outcast if they had ever been published. This was precisely what Professor Gotz-Goldstein intended the young man to do, thus bringing about the fall of the usurping director of the Brunswick Academy. But the ambitious young illustrator was developing a plan of his own. It had occurred to him that it would be more profitable for him to blackmail Professor Mothorheym instead of toppling him. As it turned out, however, he was not to succeed in this. Alerted by the 'information wanted' ad, which had not escaped his notice, Mothorheym had heard about the inquirer's visit to Professor G-G through his agents in the Colony – none other than Worldchild and Kneerider. Following his orders, they seized the young illustrator in the homeland and delivered him to Frau Suse's clinic (from which, according to the latest information, he had escaped, a mental wreck after brainwashing, through the fairy-tale theme park attached to the clinic). Corrupt as they were, Worldchild and Knee-rider had not handed over to their client the incriminating material on Mothorheym they found on the young man, but had simply sold it on to Landolfi, who was also interested in that kind of thing. The director of the Distance Learning Academy accepted their explanation that it had been burnt.

The name of the ex-official illustrator and Buckauer specialist was, of course, Sondergeld.

All this was backed up by incontrovertible evidence in the form of statements, certificates, copies, photographs etc. The file even contained a note of Sondergeld's engagement as poster-painter for Scherer-Dextry's freak show, an engagement which he had been prevented from taking up by his internment. Reuben just had to keep this file, *he* must blackmail Mothorheym with it!

Grete still hadn't come back. As quickly as he could, Reuben threw the Mothorheym file, a bottle of rum, a few high-denomination banknotes, bread and cheese into a travelling bag Grete had left lying around. With repeated cautious glances over his shoulder, he crept to the front door. He could hear Grete crashing about and swearing somewhere on the upper floor. Probably she couldn't find a big enough suitcase. Reuben left the house and the district at a run. He was wondering how he was going to carry out his plan. If only he could come of age! Then no one would come looking for him. He could leave the Colony and find out whether his parents had left him anything, the house, for example. That would have been an ideal base for his blackmailing operation. But as a lifelong seventeen-year-old?

'Oh God,' he thought, 'and I'm going to have to die some day as well.'

Epilogue

On 17 Parasumi of the following year Liliencron, who was actually a specialist in the cremation rites of Colony seals, submitted the following petition to his superiors:

For the last week I have had as my guest Herr Egner, a former writer on matters appertaining to musical recordings. This gentleman has told me of a large white poodle which, out in the inaccessible jungle of the Colony, runs a radio station playing aboriginal music all around the clock on sound-storage units resembling frozen potato cakes. The aforementioned Herr Egner appeared thoroughly plausible and even produced a few powerful drawings in evidence.

I herewith most humbly beg permission, after completion of my present research, which will shortly be brought to a successful conclusion, to be allowed to subject the abovementioned poodle and its music station to a programme of scientific investigation. I also request that the assignment of an official illustrator be dispensed with. Hecht, of whose secondment I was notified over a year ago, has still not reported for duty. I have come to an agreement with Herr Egner, who is under a publication ban in the homeland and therefore in need of a new source of income, for him to provide the necessary drawings (including those of the cremation rites of seals). I can personally vouch for the fact that Herr Egner, who while still a child created a full-colour handbook of medicine (in one single day), possesses a rough but ready talent with pen and pencil. However, to employ this talent over any length of time he has to fight back massive revulsion. To support him in this it will be necessary to dose him regularly with rum. I am therefore also indenting for several puncheons or hogsheads of old Jamaica.

God bless our lords and masters.

Amen, amen, amen.

The author would like to thank Benjamin Péret, Louis Flamel, Hans Prinzhorn, Oliver Sacks, Hoimar von Ditfurth, Bernd Rauschenbach, Gerhard Henschel, D. Baird, Joachim Blaschzyk, Helmut Tscherpel, Dietmar Leistikov, Harry Oberheinrich, the EGO-Man of Braunlage and Marie-Louise Tanguy.

German Literature from Dedalus

Dedalus features German Literature in translation in its programme of contemporary and classic European fiction and in its anthologies.

Androids from Milk – Eugen Egner £7.99
Undine – Fouqué £6.99
The Life of Courage – Grimmelshausen £6.99
Simplicissimus – Grimmelshausen £10.99
The Great Bagarozy – Helmut Krausser £7.99
The Other Side – Alfred Kubin £9.99
The Road to Darkness – Paul Leppin £7.99
The Angel of the West Window – Gustav Meyrink £9.99
The Golem – Gustav Meyrink £6.99
The Green Face – Gustav Meyrink £7.99
The Opal (& other stories) – Gustav Meyrink £7.99
Walpurgisnacht – Gustav Meyrink £6.99
The White Dominican – Gustav Meyrink £6.99
The Architect of Ruins – Herbert Rosendorfer £8.99
Letters Back to Ancient China – Herbert Rosendorfer £9.99
Stephanie – Herbert Rosendorfer £7.99

Anthologies featuring German Literature in translation:
The Dedalus Book of Austrian Fantasy – editor M. Mitchell £10.99
The Dedalus Book of German Decadence – editor R. Furness £9.99
The Dedalus Book of Surrealism – editor M. Richardson £9.99
Myth of the World: Surrealism 2 – editor M. Richardson £9.99
The Dedalus Book of Medieval Literature – editor B. Murdoch £9.99

Forthcoming titles include:
The Dedalus Book of German Fantasy: the Romantic and Beyond – editor M. Raraty £10.99

Faster Than Light – John Lucas

ARE YOU WORRIED ABOUT THE WAY THE
UNIVERSE IS GOING? OF COURSE YOU ARE!

Why are the Galaxy's wealthiest and most powerful inhabit-
ants plotting to destroy the entire universe, and replace it with
a smaller and more convenient reality of their own construction? What happens when an entire society devotes itself to
alcoholic excess, elevating the pursuit of inebriation above all
other goals? And is it really possible that the most ruthlessly
successful organisation in the whole of space and time could
be outwitted by two young humans, members of a species
previously regarded as noteworthy only for the inexplicable
enthusiasm with which it destroys the ecosystems on which
its own survival depends? Answers to all these questions and
more can be found in this unusual and dazzlingly funny novel.

Blending exuberant inventiveness with subtle satire, *Faster
Than Light* is a novel that will appeal not just to fans of
humorous science fiction, but to anyone looking for a quirky
and original read.

£8.99 ISBN 1 903517 11 7 252p paperback

Letters Back to Ancient China – Herbert Rosendorfer

Winner of The Schlegel Tieck German Translation Prize.

"A 10th-century Chinese mandarin travels forward in time, and writes letters home reporting on the strange land of 'Zha-ma-ni' in which he is surrounded by giants with big noses, and frightened by the iron carriages called 'mo-tao-ka'. We gradually realise that he is in present-day Munich, and the hapless voyager's encounters with modern life and love, make delightful reading."
   Scotland on Sunday

Letters Back to Ancient China has sold over two million copies in Germany and is seen as one of the masterpieces of contemporary German Literature.

£9.99 ISBN 1 873982 97 6 274p paperback

The Cat – Pat Gray

"Gray's reworking of the *Animal Farm* concept brings in a post-Thatcherite twist. Having peacefully co-existed with his friends Mouse and Rat (the latter carries a briefcase and wears Italian suits), the Cat's owners suddenly leave him to fend for himself. He then has to fall back on feline instincts, placating the furry packed lunches which surround him with promises of consumer goods and burrow ownership. A stylish and witty parable for the Nineties."
   Scotland on Sunday

£6.99 ISBN 1 873982 08 9 124p B. Format

Stephanie – Herbert Rosendorfer

"An elegant, elegiac novel, its titular character goes back to a past life in which she is a Spanish duchess who has murdered her husband. The book's first half, narrated by her brother, tells of the start of Stephanie's strange experience and her eventual disappearance from the present, to which she returns only to die of cancer. The second is composed of letters written by Stephanie, in 1761, to her brother. The conceit sounds trite, yet it works well. Characters are evoked economically, and the claustrophobic world to which Stephanie regresses is detailed deftly and dispassionately."

   Scotland on Sunday

"Her story is interwoven most skilfully with her 20th century life, which holds strange parallels and reflections and allows Rosendorfer some acute and occasionally darkly comic, social comment. This is a quality book from a first-rate mind of considerable sophistication. Dedalus is to be thanked for introducing us to Herbert Rosendorfer."

   Elizabeth Hawksley in The Historical Novel Review

Mike Mitchell's translation was shortlisted for The Shlegel Tieck German Translation Prize

£7.99 ISBN 1 873982 17 8 153p paperback

The Great Bagarozy – Helmut Krausser

"Psychiatrist Cora has a new patient who is obsessed with opera diva Maria Callas. Cora's life is at a crisis point: bored of her tax consultant husband and struggling with professional failure, she finds her new patient fascinating – and also dangerously attractive. She falls in love with him, but he refuses to have an affair. He claims to be the Devil and to have inhabited Callas's black poodle – is he quite simply mad? Then he disappears but Cora rediscovers him performing in variety as The Great Bagarozy. An exhilarating blend of reality and the supernatural, this is one of the most acclaimed German novels of recent years."

The Good Book Guide

"The cultures of psychiatry and celebrity worship are memorably skewered in this ingenious fantasy of satanic possession and perhaps delusion, a 1997 novel by a prize-winning and critically acclaimed German writer now making his American debut. A brilliant work. Let's have more of Krausser's fiction, please."

Kirkus Reviews

"First published in Germany in 1997 and now well translated into English by Mike Mitchell, it is a vivid and mischevious fantasy, fast-paced and often wickedly funny"

Ian Brunskill in The Times

£7.99 ISBN 1 873982 04 6 153p paperback

The Adventures of the Ingenious Alfanhui –
Rafael Sanchez Ferlosio

"In his dedication, Ferlosio describes this exquisite fantasy novel, first published in 1952 and now beautifully translated into English as a 'story full of true lies.' Much honored in his native Spain, Ferlosio is a fabulist comparable to Jorge Borges and Italo Calvino, as well as Joan Mirò and Salvador Dali. Cervantes comes to mind. Ferlosio's prose is effortlessly evocative. A chair puts down roots and sprouts 'a few green branches and some cherries,' while a paint-absorbing tree becomes a 'marvelous botanical harlequin.' Later, Alfanhui sets off on a tour of Castile, meeting his aged grandmother 'who incubated chicks in her lap and had a vine trellis of muscatel grapes and who never died.' This is a haunting adult reverie on life and beauty and as such will appeal to discriminating readers."
Starred review in Publisher's Weekly

"Trees with feathers for leaves, birds with leaves for feathers, lizards that turn into gold, rivers of blood and transparent horses – these are just some of the magical occurrences in this enchanting fairytale. This book of 'wild ideas' and 'true lies' is a kaleidoscopic celebration of the natural world, and a poetic parable on the passage from innocence to experience."
Lisa Allardice in The Independent on Sunday

". . . what keeps things moving are the vivid imagery, and the truly fantastic wonders described so vividly. A strikingly different sort of fantasy, more for fans of the surreal and magical realism than of the usual genre."
Carolyn Cushman in Locus

£8.99 ISBN 1 873982 59 3 199p paperback